Mrs. Hornstien

Mrs. Hornstien

A NOVEL

FREDRICA WAGMAN

HENRY HOLT AND COMPANY • NEW YORK

Henry Holt and Company, Inc.
Publishers since 1866
115 West 18th Street
New York, New York 10011

Henry Holt® is a registered trademark of
Henry Holt and Company, Inc.

Published in Canada by Fitzhenry & Whiteside Ltd.,
195 Allstate Parkway, Markham, Ontario L3R 4T8

Library of Congress Cataloging-in-Publication Data
Wagman, Fredrica.
Mrs. Hornstien : a novel / Fredrica Wagman.
        p.   cm.
        I. Title
PS3573.A36M77   1997   96-52528
813'.54—dc21   CIP

ISBN 0-8050-4956-8

DESIGNED BY KELLY SOONG

Printed in the United States of America
All first editions are printed on acid-free paper. °

1   3   5   7   9   10   8   6   4   2

for my mother,
for Mary Scullion,
and for Harriet Wasserman,
with gratitude and love

"It took a lifetime to squeeze the slave out of me, drop by drop by drop."

ANTON CHEKHOV

Part I

∽∽ I remember the first time we met as though it were yesterday.

She was old and massive with great shoulders and heavy breasts as she came toward me then, so long ago, with such enormous eagerness—or was it simply a need, as I think about it now, to love someone.

Her name was Golda Hornstien and she lived in a palatial apartment high over Rittenhouse Square that had the whole zodiac in the vaulted ceiling of the library, white marble stairs, mahogany walls, and in every room of that enormous place, everywhere you looked, were huge pieces of black sculpture and gigantic paintings framed in swirls of heavy carved gold wood with little brass lights on top of them, making the whole place a maze of posh old world glamour. It was a richness I had never seen the likes of, but then, I was only seventeen years old that night, so I hadn't seen much of anything as I stood next to her son, staring at her.

3

"Mother," Albert said quietly as he held my hand, "this is Marty. Marty," he said, as I felt his grip tightening, "this is my mother."

"How do you do, Mrs. Hornstien," I remember saying as I put out my hand. It was a long time ago, almost thirty-five years, but I remember the tan cashmere sweater set she wore that night with the triple strand of graduated pearls and the large man's Hamilton watch with the stretch metal band pushed high up on her arm, over her sweater sleeve, like it happened yesterday.

That she was beautiful came in the next wave of impressions that swept over me as I stood staring at her deeply lined face, at her long, straight white hair, at her eyes that were the lightest blue I had ever seen. They were summer blue the way you'd imagine the colors of the sea and the sky in a picture poster of summertime. She had high cheekbones that looked almost Mongol, a small straight nose and big teeth that flashed when she smiled, making her dimples become lost in all the deep craggy lines of her face. But most of all it was a certain grandness she had. Mrs. Hornstien was, in fact, a smallish woman, but there was something enormous about her. A great raw power shot out of her in just the way she carried herself—her enormous spirit leaped out the instant she smiled to swamp all the sculpture and all the paintings and anyone who was standing there as she came toward me that first time and hugged me like she had been waiting for me for years.

Men have contempt for the kind of woman who loves too easily and too much—the kind of woman who has a secret hungry longing that floats around scanning for something to attach to, and looking back, I realize now that for Mrs. Hornstien I was that thing, only I didn't understand this then. Then I couldn't imagine what there was about me that made her take to me so fast. In those days I was a strange, quiet kid with swarthy skin, too much kinky hair and so shy I could barely say a word, but between Mrs. Hornstien and me something clicked. I liked her right off the bat in the same way she liked me, which was almost the way that Albert did, which I also didn't understand, but as I've said, I was only seventeen years old that night, so I didn't understand much of anything as we stood smiling at each other in the Moorish archway of the library while our eyes became two sets of bizarre instruments that could discern and detect everything there was about the other just by looking.

⦿⦿ "Dear, *dear* child," Mrs. Hornstien beamed as she took my hand. "May I give you a cup of tea?" she smiled, as she looped her arm in mine and began leading me toward the kitchen.

And as I followed, my heart was pounding from knowing that I'd soon have to say something to this looming person who seemed to me then more like an apartment house or a bank or a department store than a regular woman. She kept beaming at me so broadly it felt like giant floodlights had been turned directly on my face, making me freeze in my tracks, like a deer caught in the glaring headlights of a car.

"MARTY!" she said. "What kind of name is THAT?" she laughed as if to say "POO! That's not a name—That's not ANYTHING!"

"How old are you?" she said, "and what does your daddy do?" she asked as we passed out of the huge front hall with its enormous paintings and great pieces of gigantic sculpture into the dining room on our way to the kitchen, and in looking back, how the dining room that night, even though I only saw it for a flash and in almost total darkness, became one of the great memories of my life.

Everything in there was Venetian glass and smoky mirrored walls and gray satin—the drapes with their heavy drooping tiebacks with gray satin balls hanging from them like Christmas toys, the shimmering gray satin dining room chairs lined up on both sides of the table like little soldiers waiting at attention, the ceiling that was covered in thick gray satin and the gray grasscloth walls that were gleaming in the dark in a kind of eerie incandescence like the last rays of daylight peering out through gathering black clouds so that for a moment the whole world looks a kind of silver before the storm, and in the middle of it all, floating over the long glass table, a huge crystal chandelier wrapped in gauze making it look like a ghost or a phantom or like the spirit of some ancient soul hovering up near the ceiling who saw and heard and remembered everything.

"We raised all the children right here in this house," Mrs. Hornstien said. "The boys had their bar mitzvah luncheons and their graduation dinners right here," she said, "and my daughter Doris was married

7

right here with over three hundred guests at the wedding, and oh my God!" she said, "the entertaining we used to do—am I right son?" Mrs. Hornstien asked Albert as we were all sailing onward toward the kitchen, "didn't we have the most wonderful parties in this house, and all the luncheons I used to give and all the teas. I gave the weddings for my three nieces here as well as their engagement parties and all their wedding showers and they were the most beautiful parties you could ever imagine—am I right son?" Mrs. Hornstien asked Albert.

"Of course you're right. Whatever the Boss Lady says is always right. Everyone knows that," Albert answered with a kind of odd edge to his voice that I can still remember.

"When I was a girl," Mrs. Hornstien went on blithely as though she hadn't heard him, "I came from very poor circumstances. We came to this country with nothing, and I mean *nothing*!" she said. "We were so poor we only had four fingers on each hand," she laughed as she gave me a nudge with the elbow of the arm that was looped in mine.

"I never wanted jewels," she said, "not that I didn't get them," she laughed as she nudged me again with her elbow, "but I never cared about them one way or the other, like I never cared about furs or big fancy cars or designer clothes. All I ever dreamed of having was a beautiful home where we could raise our family, because a home," she said, "is the closest thing to a human being in the way it holds you in its warmth and protects you and soothes you. So when we saw this place," she said as she pushed open the swinging kitchen door, "I said to Daddy THIS IS IT — This is the home I've dreamed of all my life. This is where we have to raise our children so they'll be proud to bring home their little school friends, and be proud to have their parties here, and all their big important celebrations as they get older — am I right Daddy? Isn't that what I said the first time we saw this place even before all the walls were up?" she asked little Oscar Hornstien, who was walking with Albert just behind us as we headed into the soft brown light of the kitchen — "Well, Daddy," Mrs. Hornstien asked, "isn't that what I said?"

"That's what you said," I heard a voice pipe up, and then I heard Albert add, "whatever the Boss Lady says!" with the same little sarcastic edge. What's going on around here I remember thinking. Poor Mrs. Hornstien, I remember saying to myself. But in those days I didn't make a sound because in those days to give even the smallest hint that I was feeling something even slightly off would have been like crossing some invisible line I would never dare to cross because who was I, I would have asked myself—what did I know, and anyhow, what business was it of mine what went on between Albert and his mother, I would have told myself at the first hint of any impulse to stand up for Mrs. Hornstien about what seemed to me then the fact that her son was picking on her. In those days I was too afraid of making a fool of myself by saying something wrong so I never said anything. And that silence caused by a fear of being humiliated pervaded every corner of my life every waking minute of every day. In fact, if you were to ask me who I was, I'd say I was a living, walking breathing fear of being humiliated, so I never said two words to anyone unless I had to.

In school, that is, on the days I was allowed to go to school, because my mother had a terror of letting me out of her sight, the children used to shout "cat got your tongue" out on the playground hoping to make me speak, but I'd never give in, or else they'd call me "mute head" because I would talk to no one except another quiet kid who sat behind me whose name was Stephen Berg. Otherwise, I answered only the questions the teachers asked. I never laughed with the other kids or joked around or shared secrets, and at home it was pretty much the same. I never said anything to anyone unless I had to.

I grew up in a suburb of Philadelphia called Bala Cynwyd, a simple place with semidetached Victorian houses that had stone walls in front with privet hedges on top of them, and there were big front porches and short lawns dark from too many trees so the grass would never grow out front, and on all the porches there used to be white metal porch furniture that rocked.

The school I went to was set in the middle of a small green field surrounded on all sides by what seemed to me then like some kind of enchanted forest, but in fact, all it was was a wooded patch behind the railroad tracks that was filled with trees and dead tree trunks and moss and wild growing things and broken sunlight and the constant sound of birds that would fill me with so much joy every time I went in there that tears would come.

When I was seventeen, which was the year I met Albert, I used to think a lot about God and about the weather which always seemed like a gift, and about the wind and its ferocious power. I used to think about the way flowers grew everywhere inside those woods and how marvelous it was on a summer afternoon to sit in there on the big rocks beside the creek with my feet dangling in the water. I didn't think about the way Albert picked on his mother because I didn't want to think about anything that might cast even a wisp of a cloud over the immense happiness I was feeling. It was wonderful to be sitting on the big rocks beside the creek thinking about Albert Hornstien or looking at him in the kitchen of his mother's palace high over Rittenhouse Square, knowing nothing then, not wanting to, and yet expecting everything.

꩜ The kitchen of Mrs. Hornstien's apartment was an artless little secret all its own. It was a somber milk-brown place where everything old and dingy melted into the brownness all around it. But as dreary as it was with old red linoleum furniture, chalky milk-brown walls, and a decrepit old black stove, this was the place where everyone gathered every night to drink their tea and eat their ginger-snaps in peace, as if the absence of all the glamour, art, and marble was a relief.

Mrs. Hornstien knew that Albert and I were going to be married almost the first moment she laid eyes on me. It was an instinct she had, or else it's a sense most mothers have at certain times when they seem to be receiving information that nobody else seems to have any indication of, so she was very curious about my family—Who were we, she wanted to know, and in the next breath she wanted to know if we were German Jewish or if we were Russian Jewish because this was the silent line that divides the high-class Jews from the low-class Jews which I knew all about because I used to hear it all the time at my grandfather's house.

According to my Grandfather Kohn, German Jews were all snobs who looked down their noses on everyone who wasn't German, never gave a cent to any Jewish cause, hated Israel, never traveled there, weren't Zionists and never bought Israeli bonds, and according to my grandfather, Russian Jews were even worse.

True, my grandfather used to say, they were all Zionists which of course was to their credit, but they were also low-class peasants who ate with their fingers, mopped up their gravy with their bread, ran around barefooted, wore babushkas on their heads and spoke Yiddish which according to my grandfather was a humiliation to have to listen to. The fact that they supported Israel and knew how to spend was of course to their credit, except, they went too far as far as jewelry was concerned, but not as far as the Sephardic Jews, who in my grandfather's opinion were even lower on the scale than the Russian Jews, and of course no one was lower than the Polish Jews — But! According to my grandfather, our family! Now that was different!

We were American Jews, my grandfather used to beam. The old country for us was Girard Avenue across from Fairmount Park where my grandmother was born in her grandmother's living room, all of them here for generations, all of them originally from Czechoslovakia, which is neither Russia nor Germany but rather some kind of superior netherland of writers and artists and culture and history, but even that didn't matter according to Grandfather Kohn, because we had been here so long that it didn't matter where we came from. My brother Kal and I were fifth-generation American-born reformed Jews who sang the National Anthem in synagogue on the High Holy Days, and for Jews like us, there was no other country. There was no other history. We were American first and Jewish second, not the other way around like the Russian and the German Jews. But! This was only on my mother's side—on my father's side it was a different story.

As I was sitting at Mrs. Hornstien's kitchen table I was thinking how my mother's family used to call my father and his family "kikes" behind their backs which I later learned meant Russian Jews, and so, when Mrs. Hornstien took hold of my hand, flashed me another one of her gorgeous smiles and began closing in on me like an enormously good-natured octopus, I was worried that if I dared mention anything about my background, and then if it turned out that she wasn't on the same side of that invisible dividing line as I, she would instantly despise me the way my mother despised the whole Fish family.

"Now tell me dear," she said as she began warming into it, "what is your father's name and what does he do?" she asked as she flashed another one of her magic smiles.

"His name was Bernie Fish," I said. "He was a doctor," I remember telling her as I looked her dead in the eye so as not to feel the pang that either his name or his death or his life might cause in me.

"A doctor," I remember her saying offhandedly as though not impressed at all. "What kind of doctor?" she asked as she kept smiling at me.

"A regular doctor who made house calls," I answered feeling, I can still remember, like maybe a doctor wasn't good enough.

"Well, women make their fortunes through marriage, don't they dear?" she said. "A brilliant marriage for a woman is exactly the same as a man who makes a brilliant business deal," she smiled at me. "The mistake most people make is to confuse the two. Marriage is a serious business arrangement," she smiled, "while romance and love are very different

16

matters—am I right Daddy?" she smiled at little Oscar Hornstien, who was leaning against the doorjamb grinning.

"I had our Daddy," she said, as she smiled at her husband again. His arms were crossed over his white cotton shirt, no tie, no jacket. He was a small man, just an inch or so above five feet—thin, wiry and red-faced, with a shock of thick white hair as he stood grinning at every word that came out of Mrs. Hornstien's mouth.

"That's right," she said, "and together we had the WILL and the DRIVE and the AMBITION to make something of ourselves—am I right, Daddy?" she asked her husband, who stood there still leaning on the doorjamb grinning at her.

"We started out in one little room above a shirtmaker's shop on Strawberry Street," she said. "No heat! No electric lights! No running water or even a toilet to pee in. Only one freezing room, a table, two chairs, and the two of us and our WILL and our DRIVE and our AMBITION because without money you're a NOTHING," she said. "You're a NOBODY! You're a BEGGAR!

"But!" she said, "don't think for one minute that that ice-cold room we had above the shirtmaker's shop wasn't good. It was very good because that's where it all began," Mrs. Hornstien said. "We were young and we had the dream of doing and not just for ourselves but for our children and for our children's children—we wanted to give to them. That was our dream. That was what drove us.

"I'll let you in on a big secret," she said as she moved closer, "you'll always get by," she said, "if you give to your children and if they let you because doing for them is what life is all about," she said as she clutched my hand.

"It's a funny thing," she said, "but you'll see someday that your children, believe it or not, will be the biggest thrill of all. Who would have ever guessed?" she said. "With all the things we work for, or dream of having, who would ever guess that the biggest thrill of all the thrills there are is simply your child," she said as she stared up at the ceiling for a moment.

"So," she said, "as soon as we got going a little, after the orders started coming in and we could begin to hire some people to start rolling the tobacco instead of just Daddy and I up in that room when we had to wear three pair of gloves at a time, plus two mufflers around our faces—and the hats, and the coats, and so many scarves and sweaters we couldn't even count them come January and February. But," she said, "when we moved to Fifth and Arch—then," she said, "it was another life.

"When we moved to Fifth and Arch," she said, "that was the beginning of nothing we could have ever dreamed — not in our wildest imaginations.

"Today," she said, "the building on the corner of Fifth and Arch is the United States Mint building, but back in those days before Albert sold it to the government it was the first office, loading dock, and warehouse of the Horn Cigar Company Incorporated," she said, her face glowing with all the pride of their success. "And may I tell you," she beamed at me, her eyes flashing with so much excitement by then that there were almost tears, "we were then, as we are now, THE BIGGEST MANUFACTURERS OF SMALL CIGARS in the entire WORLD with or WITHOUT the help of our dear Cuban friend Mr. Fidel — am I right, son?

"Have we got good tobacco right here in Pennsylvania? And what about Virginia? And what about Kentucky? Am I right, Albert?" she asked. "Well?"

"Of course you're right, because the Boss Lady's ALWAYS RIGHT!" Albert answered as he began running water into a big copper teapot.

"And who do you think did all the books in those days?" she asked as she pulled her chair up closer to mine. "Who do you think hired every person in that place for the next thirty-four years and trained each one of them and taught each one of them everything

19

they knew and kept a good eye on each and every one of them like each and every one of them were my own CHILDREN—That's right, who else?

"And what's more," she said, "who do you think entertained each and every customer like each and every customer was ROYALTY with such exquisite gifts from only the finest shops in Philadelphia. Shops like Nan Ruskins on Walnut Street and the Rumm Store—I don't mean bribes," she said, "I mean gifts," she said—"because a gift is a weapon," she said, looking at me sternly as she clutched my hand.

"Daddy and I were so poor when we got married that Daddy couldn't afford to buy me a wedding band. Imagine!" she said. "We had to borrow a ring from Daddy's sister Fanny Lichtenstien, the big shot in the family because she was married to a dentist so of course she held this over me, but we showed her, didn't we Daddy, because when we went public in nineteen thirty-six, do you know the first thing Daddy did? He went to Cartier's in New York City and bought me the most exquisite diamond necklace I ever saw in my entire life, and do you know . . . it was made entirely of diamond wedding bands, one beside the next beside the next to form three rows that went from the base of my neck halfway down my chest. . . . Come!" she said as she shot up, "while they're making the tea, I'm going to show it to you," she said as she grabbed my arm, pulled me out of my chair and began leading me again, first out of the kitchen, then back through the darkened dining room, then back through the long front hall, up the winding flight of white marble stairs and into her bedroom . . . I shall never forget that night—not ever, I feel myself smile as I glance at my watch.

I can still see her darting around the room collecting little velvet boxes out of various dresser drawers, then dumping all the contents onto the tan satin bedspread in front of me.

Everything in Mrs. Hornstien's bedroom was tan satin—the drapes, the bedspread, all the little pillows, her low dressing-table chair and the chaise longue—and as I stood there stunned because I had never seen a room with so much satin and such exquisite little lights coming out of the walls on what looked like little crystal trees and satin drapes with another pair of long lace drapes behind them, and the button backs on the chair and on the chaise, but was nothing compared to the diamond pins and earrings and bracelets, and the necklace made of hundreds of diamond wedding bands, plus emerald things and things made of rubies and sapphires, all of them dumped out on the bed in front of me. "Sit down!" she said as she gave me a little push, and then back she went to tearing around the room and then back she came and before I knew it, all her jewelry—all of her diamonds and emeralds and rubies, all of her chains of pearls the size of marbles, and an enormous diamond ring and an even bigger emerald ring that looked like a huge hunk of bright green glass—was draped on me like gleaming junk from the five-and-ten, only bigger and brighter, as she pulled me over to her dressing table, and as I stood there looking at myself covered in Mrs. Hornstien's jewelry, it felt odd—like she was trying to bribe me, only for what reason I couldn't imagine.

And then it was all over. As if a black storm cloud had suddenly descended over her, she somberly began dismantling my decorations and even more somberly packing everything back into all the little velvet boxes and then slowly putting them back into all the various dresser drawers around the room, and then, as we began walking back to the kitchen, the great cloud broke—"He was only twenty-four years old with everything to live for," she began sobbing as she took my arm.

"He was driving too fast," she said as she began wiping her nose with the handkerchief that was tucked in her sweater sleeve. "That was what he loved," she said, "fast cars that he drove too fast. They said it happened somewhere between Nice and Monte Carlo on one of those treacherous hairpin turns. Well," she said, "they found the car two days after it happened, his neck," she said, as she struggled to compose herself, "was severed to the spine so that his body was leaning forward against the steering wheel while his head had fallen backward with his face looking up at the sky. . . . Gone!" she said. "Just like that—Done! Finished! He was gypped out of everything," she whispered. "Everything! Everything!" she said as her eyes filled up again with wide red tears, only this time they didn't spill.

"No one is indispensable except your child," she said, staring at me as she pushed open the swinging kitchen door, "and that's when grief becomes something different than anything you ever knew the meaning of," she said as she stared at me with both her hands clutching one of mine.

"That's enough, Golda!" Albert ordered her as he took the teapot off the stove and began pouring the water into her cup. "We're not going to talk about this tonight," he said as he looked at his mother.

"Yes," she said almost like a child," "we won't talk about Benjamin tonight," she smiled. "My son Albert doesn't like to talk about his brother Benjamin," she said as she looked at me, her eyes clouding up again with more red tears that didn't spill. . . . And as I sat there watching them, I was amazed at how they knew exactly how far to go so as not to spill over, as if they had been doing it that way for so long that by now she had absolutely perfected this tearless way of crying.

"On the twenty-first of May at eleven o'clock in the morning, Benjamin Hornstien took his last breath," she whispered quietly so Albert wouldn't hear.

"May I tell you something?" she whispered to me as she brought her face up close to mine, "it is we who destroy ourselves, and it is we who save ourselves, and no one else," she whispered as her eyes became red and full again.

And as I looked at her, once again it was the tears that registered as they came to a halt exactly at the edge of her eyelids—not her pain.

I sat at the kitchen table watching Mrs. Hornstien's eyes fill up and her lower lip contort in agony, but I felt nothing, and about this I've had trouble with myself, but as I've said, I was so young—too young then to know what it is to lose a child, or to get old, or to realize that soon another son was about to leave. All I knew that night was how much I wanted Mrs. Hornstien to like me as I sat staring at her pain.

∽∾ Not long after that, on one of those soft evenings in late August, the Hornstiens took Albert and me out to their country club, and as we sat on the big open porch eating dinner, for me it was like being in a dream.

All the tables that night were draped in long white skirts with candles in big glass hurricanes. The wine and water glasses were all lined up like staunch soldiers guarding heavy silver lay plates that were surrounded by a bewildering array of spoons and knives and forks, and there were white gardenias and napkins trimmed in lace, making the tables look like something out of a magazine.

The big open porch of the clubhouse where we were eating was once the porch of a white stucco mansion pitched across calm green rolling lawns with ancient oak trees and enormous weeping willows that whispered a peacefulness that floated through the night, as porcelain ladies with faces that looked like they had been ironed and their hair just so and their jewelry flashing glided onto the dance floor on the arms of suntanned men who I remember thinking all looked like smiling walnuts in white dinner jackets. And as waiters scurried with trays and the music played, it seemed like something out of colonial India, or like a page taken from a book about a dynasty from a hundred years before.

Ashmont Country Club reeked of the pride of belonging. It reeked of wealth and of peace and of summers that would roll softly into each other like an endless trail of Sunday afternoons—this bastion of the privileged class—and of their prejudices and of their ironly protected secrets, scandals, and fortunes so that finally, a dazzlingly exquisite sense of safety pervaded everything.

For Golda and Oscar Hornstien Ashmont Country Club was nothing special. You could tell just by the way they looked at the waiter, ordered dinner and then handed back their menus while for me it was like walking the line that separates excitement from terror.

On the one hand I loved being there because it was beautiful, green, soft, and rolling, with stone terraces lined with potted flowers, and a quiet and an order that pervaded everything and these were feelings I relished. Until then I had felt such things only in the public library. Nowhere else. Never outside, and never while I was eating dinner, so that Ashmont Country Club was almost a place of unreality to me. Here was a fairy tale that wasn't quite a fairy tale. It was a real place where I could stop, breathe a little and then bask for just a minute in a luxurious softness I had never known.

On the other hand, Ashmont Country Club was like being tested every moment I was there. My background didn't include that kind of opulence, any more than it included knowing which fork to use with the fish or which spoon was supposed to be used for dessert.

On top of that, the Hornstiens, who had their eye on me the whole time they were eating, never put their knives down once. I noticed out of the corner of my eye that they kept using their knives during the whole meal not only to cut their food but also to push their food onto their forks, while I was taught that you had to put your knife down every time you were finished cutting and then put your fork back into the hand you used to eat with or else my father would hit the roof.

My family had fallen on hard times when I met

Albert. Once they had great wealth that came with all the trimmings. But that was long before I was born. Now there were only stories—broken sets of china and crystal from better times, and my father hovering over the dinner table more like a drill sergeant than a relative. One wrong remark or one little look he didn't like, or if my fork wasn't exactly according to what he decided was correct, and he would fly into a rage that made my brother and me freeze. Then by some magic trick, I would find myself floating up near the ceiling, out of my body and out of his narrow range of madness.

About how to turn myself into a speck and then disappear I knew everything there was to know, like I knew how to slink down so low in my chair at the table he'd barely notice I was there, or how to stop all sounds including even the sound of my own breathing—about things like that I was a master because I knew that that was the only way to sidestep a father whose whole being seemed to be one that yelled and banged fists and shot glaring looks. But about which fork to use with the fish, about white tennis outfits and eating lunch on a big open porch where all you had to do was sign when you were done—about things like that I didn't have a clue because things like that could only be part of a world of unimaginable dignity—a civilized world of safety and protection which was a world I knew nothing about whatever.

That night Mrs. Hornstien wore a blue chiffon evening gown almost the color of her eyes with that same triple strand of luminous yellow pearls, but instead of the man's Hamilton watch pushed high up on her arm with the stretch metal band, that night she wore a thick diamond bracelet and a huge round diamond ring that was so full of life that I could see it sparkling all the way from the stone wall down beside the swimming pool where Albert and I were sitting after dinner, deciding whether or not to go in for a swim.

In those early years, I'm thinking as I glance at my watch again, Albert was very thin with tan bony ankles that I remember thinking were "princely."

When he crossed his legs, which he always did as soon as he sat down, he took on a loose kind of swankiness, and with the addition of those bony, tanned, princely ankles—no socks and his brown alligator loafers with the little tassels—something immensely appealing came across.

His looks, which were sort of the classy gangster type, were accented by skin that was pockmarked and craggy, giving him a kind of weatherbeaten look.

But it was his great simplicity, the large features of his big honest face, and his eyes which reflected so much kindness that became a refuge for me from the first instant I laid eyes on him.

Albert was twelve years older than I, which took him out of the boyfriend category and made him something more, something grown and established— something powerful. From the beginning Albert was bigger than life to me. No one can own another person, but at seventeen you think you can just like you think you can put into words the mute depths within yourself that are eternally wordless.

At seventeen you think the chasm between two people that can never be bridged is bridgeable—that all you have to do is do it. But it can't be done, just like you can't own anyone, or word the wild depths that are forever a haunting echo of some other song. It's all too fragmented and in parts that never fall into place—this business between two people just like you think that if you die the other person will stop living too but he won't, nothing stops and no one because the human spirit, which is more or less indestructible, can't be owned, put into words, or captured, only you don't know any of this at seventeen as you hunger for a completeness that can never be.

After dinner that night, as Albert and I were sitting on the low stone wall down beside the swimming pool deciding whether or not to go in for a swim, Albert took a little black velvet box out of his pocket, opened it and then put a diamond ring on my finger. It was big, square, colorless, perfect, and so long it almost came to my second knuckle, and as I stared at it my heart began to sink. Who was I, I was thinking—even to look at such a thing. Where did I, Marty Fish, come to such a thing that literally took my breath away, and as I kept staring at it I remember I was thinking of my mother—how could I explain to Albert that my mother had just become a widow, and even though she was scraping together the best she could, my father's death left us penniless and over our heads in debt, so how could I, under circumstances like this, even show a ring like this to her when things at home were so bad—that's all I could think of, nothing else—that's all that kept moving through my mind as Albert was asking me for the second time and then for the third to marry him.

၄၄ Because of my mother, either my fear of her or my concern for how she would take it, either way, I was too uncomfortable to wear the ring, so it was put in Albert's safe where it stayed until after we were married, and if Mrs. Hornstien had a great fondness for me in the beginning, she turned on me with that much violence the moment she learned that Albert and I were engaged.

"SHE'S A REAL LITTLE NOTHING!" Albert said she started yelling, her hands clenched and her face crimson with fury.

"THIS LITTLE WHOEVER SHE THINKS SHE IS is telling me—GOLDA HORNSTIEN—to move over because she's the big cheese now—Albert," she said, "I could tell just by the way she looked at me the first time we met that she was declaring WAR!

"So! This is the reward for a lifetime of love and of

care and a million sleepless nights—is it? To just be dumped like you're yesterday's news," Mrs. Hornstien was reported to have said with her hands still clenched and her face the color of a beet.

"So!" she said. "This is the way it goes—this is what happens—I'm not on top anymore—is that what you're telling me? Well, Albert, I can tell you something too. This announcement you're overwhelming me with at this stage of my life feels exactly like an amputation! Your telling me that you're getting married feels like my right leg is being cut off at the hip without a drop of anesthesia," Albert said she said brazenly, as though she had the right to simply say anything that came into her head.

"Please, Albert," she was reported to have begun begging him as she unclenched her hands and started wiping her nose and eyes with a handkerchief, "I beg you, son," she said, "slow down, take your time, get to know this girl, find out something about her family because you marry all of them, Albert, not just the girl—you marry every single rotten one of them so you better know who they are, what kind of people, if anyone has a prison record, let's have the office investigate a little bit before you decide anything so fast because remember son, the apple never falls far from the tree no matter what kind of tree it is so you just want to find a nice good girl who will never hurt you son, because if she has no character she'll not only break your heart but she'll also break your bankbook and take my word, I can tell just by looking that this girl has NO CHARACTER WHATSOEVER! But you won't listen to me will you, Albert," she asked him, "because no one listens to me anymore.

"You and Daddy give each other looks that you don't think I see—looks that say I'm not that sharp anymore, looks that say I'm getting dotty and not making sense but I see every look," she said, "I also know that you and Daddy think I've begun to talk too much, that I've begun to ramble like an old lady who repeats herself, no judgment anymore, just blabber and don't think I haven't noticed that you and Daddy don't need me anymore, lately I feel like I'm even in the way around here like you secretly want to bundle me up in a big fur coat and put a blue hat on my head and then sit me out on the terrace with the colored girl, well, I suppose I have to face this too like I have to face the fact that eventually I'm going to lose out to that scrawny little whatever she is so I tell myself, lose with grace, Golda, because this is the way life is—Loss upon Loss upon Loss until you have nothing left, not a tooth in your head or a hair on your crotch, except maybe three or four straight ones like a catfish's chin. But I tell you, whether you think I'm crazy or not, I've seen that type a thousand times, quiet and mousy on the outside, but underneath she knows EXACTLY what she's doing, Albert," his mother was purported to have said, "I want to tell you right now that you are dealing here with a TARANTULA who may not LOOK old enough to be that smart, but take my word, she knows a good thing when she sees one, don't kid yourself Albert," she told him, "for this girl this is a BUSINESS DEAL as plain as the nose on your face because your little girlfriend with those little squinched-up eyes and those scrawny toothpick legs LOVES MONEY MORE THAN SHE LOVES LIFE!

"One look at that face shooting daggers at me before she even said HELLO, and in one second flat I could see that you were dealing with a real, bona fide, first-class GOLD DIGGER!" his mother told him, "and the minute you walk down the aisle with that mousy little NOTHING with those eyebrows that somebody should take a tweezer to, and such scrawny ARMS AND LEGS! MY GOD! What's the MATTER? Hasn't she ever had a square meal in her LIFE! Well, son," Mrs. Hornstien was reported to have said, "this scrawny little NOTHING is going to get you good and then watch out, she'll start spending like there's no tomorrow because it's always the ones who never had a thing that can never get enough. "They're the ones, mark my words," she said, "who spend like it's spigot water because once they have the law on their side—WATCH OUT!

"First comes all the clothes they never had, then the furs and the jewels and the cars and then the houses, and I don't mean just one or two—I mean three or four MANSIONS with all of them decorated to the hilt by someone like Bennett and Judith Weinstock Interiors in nothing but the finest English country with imported toilet paper spindles and china export bathtub faucets or else God forbid, how could they show their faces out at the club?

"Albert dear," his mother had begged him, "all I'm asking you to do is wait, do some checking, get to know what kind of character she has, is she or isn't she after everything she can get her hands on, and while you're waiting to get some important answers I'll have a chance to catch my breath a little too, let me have a minute to get used to all of this, one son I've already lost, and now my other is about to go not even two years later, Albert," she said, "it takes too much out of me all at once, the Bible says 'Honor

Thy Mother And Thy Father That Their Days May Be Long Upon The Earth The Lord Has Given Them,' son," she said, "I'm not asking you to give her up, all I'm asking you to do is honor me just this once by waiting a little while—tell me—is that so much to ask?"

"You asked Ben to wait and he did and what good did it do him?" Albert told his mother. "I've waited twenty-nine years for Marty and I'm not waiting anymore," he said.

Then Albert said his mother turned, went up the stairs, called Catherine to come pull down the blinds, close the drapes and turn back her bed. Then Albert said she got in bed, had Catherine turn down the lights and close the door behind her and according to Albert, Mrs. Hornstien stayed in there with the curtains drawn and all the lights turned low for over a week.

The night Albert asked me to marry him, Mrs. Hornstien and I had just gone to the ladies' room after dinner. I remember it seemed like such a long walk that night because she took me through the lobby first, out the front door of the clubhouse, across the driveway, and then back in again through the women's locker room which in fact was right next to the open porch where we were having dinner. All she would have had to do was walk two steps away from the porch and in the entrance of the women's locker room and we would have been right there, but before she knew Albert and I were going to be married, she wanted all the time she could have with me—all she wanted then was to take me around on little tours introducing me to everyone we'd meet like she was showing me off as well as showing everything off to me.

That night as we were walking, I remember thinking what a peaceful place even the women's locker room was. Everyone was gone. All the lights were turned off, leaving the green metal lockers against the walls still and silent with the worn wooden benches empty in front of them, nothing out of place, not a hair, not a shadow, with all the golf shoes lined up on the wooden racks along the walls waiting dolefully and with endless patience to be cleaned.

The sinks and showers were still another stretch of yet more peace and luxury. Above the empty sinks was a shelf with bowls of cotton balls and hair dryers and brushes and black combs in cannisters of thin blue water. There were cans of hair spray up there and boxes of Tampax and baskets full of soaps and talcs and little packs of aspirin — anything you'd ever want or need right there waiting — which to me again had that same strange quality of make-believe, another storybook room that was about still more luxury and leisure — that's what I was thinking as Mrs. Hornstien and I were walking arm in arm while she talked about her son Benjamin.

Every word from the moment we left the dinner table, every word as we were walking, every word while we were in our separate toilet stalls next to each other peeing, and then standing side by side while we were washing our hands and drying them on white linen hand towels, was about the son she lost out on a road she could never imagine, no less forgive or ever forget, even though she had never seen it. How he was only seventeen when he went to Yale and twenty-one when he started Harvard Law School, how good-looking he was and the strings of gorgeous women from only the very best families. But of course he had to go and pick a shiksa showgirl (or was she a model or a hairdresser—she couldn't quite remember), who of course Mrs. Hornstien would not receive, and who, THANK GOD! she said, he never married.

All of this not twenty minutes before Albert asked me to marry him, which is why I remember it so clearly. I remember how perfect the timing was because it allowed my hands to be immaculate when Albert put the diamond on my finger.

If I didn't wear the ring until after we were married because I was worried then about my mother's reaction to it, at least for the moment that I had it on my finger before Albert put it in the vault, my hands were spotless. That's what I was thinking about—not about what Mrs. Hornstien was saying or the pain of her unbearable tragedy—all I was thinking about then were my hands and that they were clean.

In a funny way it's like it all happened only yesterday—the first time I met Mrs. Hornstien here in this palatial apartment high over Rittenhouse Square and how we stood in the archway just over there eyeing each other like our eyes were microscopes—how I walked with her that night into that magical gray satin dining room for the first time—how I sat on her bed as she put all her jewelry on me and how her eyes filled with sad red tears as she spoke about the son she lost, and then how Albert's eyes filled with tears of joy just a few minutes later as he gave me the ring and asked me to marry him—the jumble of events, the wild roll of the dice, I smile wistfully as I glance at my watch again, remembering.

And at the same time, it's like it all happened some timeless time ago—eons ago, as I glance once more at my watch wondering why Albert's already an hour late.

Seven days later Mrs. Hornstien got out of bed, called Catherine to come in and open the drapes, raise the blinds, bring over the telephone while she got out her book, and then she proceeded to call everyone in the family to tell them that Albert was going to be married.

Next, she called Nan Ruskin, which was then the most exclusive shop in Philadelphia, got hold of her furrier, Mr. Weiss, ordered a full-length gray mink coat — male skins only — had them wrap it in a big silver box with a big silver bow. Then she had Crump, who had been driving for them for over thirty years, take her, her daughter, Doris Taxin, Doris's husband Stanley, Albert's father little Oscar Hornstien, and the gray mink coat to my mother's house in Bala Cynwyd.

The house where I grew up was a dark Victorian semidetached with a dark front porch, a grassless short front lawn with overgrown ivy attached to all the walls all over the house.

Inside, the walls downstairs were all painted pea green with white woodwork, all the oversized furniture was pea green, most of it with its stuffing coming out, and all the Chinese rugs that were given to my mother by an uncle who was in the liquidating business were worn down to their spotty white naps.

The tables on the whole left side of the house if you were facing the front door needed a book under at least one leg to keep the table from tipping because the house tilted so badly on that side that the tables over there always had all their drawers half open.

On the walls old prints of birds and big needlepoints in thin gold frames that my mother picked up in dusty little antique shops on Pine Street hung above the weathered furniture, which was either upholstered in threadbare pea green damask or else covered in baggy, worn-out, pea green cotton slipcovers, and it wasn't just because my mother loved pea green, which indeed she did, but it was also because she didn't know what else to do with all the dark drafty space that was in that house, which, even though it was a semidetached, was enormous. My mother was a fierce little bantam chicken, combative

43

and high-spirited, who had her own personal ethic based entirely on a feeling that she was entitled to everything under the sun, and this point of view forced her sometimes to steal, lie, and throw fits.

The Friday night dinner the Hornstiens were coming to our house to have was always a thick blur of food, whiskey, too much heat from all the sizzling radiators and a big loosening of affection bordering on maudlin sentimentality that to me was always excruciatingly embarrassing. When I was younger I used to want to die when I'd see all my uncles and my grandfather after a couple of gins begin banging their fists on the table swearing how they'd die for one another "without batting an eye." But the food, which my grandmother and her maid Rosina Washington prepared—the sauerkraut soup and the potato kugel, the brisket, the chicken poprikoff, the fried eggplant, and my grandmother's famous cauliflower in lobster sauce which was my favorite, plus a sweet potato pudding that had a heavy marshmallow crust that became all brown and chewy as it baked, a salad dressing made of cream cheese, garlic, and olive oil and all the sweet butter rolls, the rye bread with seeds, and the incredible desserts like Rosina Washington's coconut custard pie, her lopsided lemon meringue pie, a chocolate chip hazelnut cake from the Swiss Pastry Shop on Nineteenth Street, and finally the chocolate brownies that were my mother's masterpiece contribution would lure me back week after week despite how embarrassing my family's behavior was to me as I was growing up.

But the night the Hornstiens were coming things were altered dramatically. That night my mother made a chicken cacciatore dish which was the only time I remember my mother ever making anything besides brownies in my life. The guest list was expanded that Friday night to include not only the usual aunts and uncles, my brother Kal, my cousins, my grandparents, and my mother, but that night my mother invited her closest friends to get a look at the Hornstiens — my fake aunt Sylvia Eshelman, who was a flamboyant gynecologist with dyed red hair and a tremendous bust, and her husband, Dr. Eshelman, who was my mother's lover.

Everyone was on his best behavior that night, including Dr. Eshelman, whose behavior was usually unspeakable, which meant there were no filthy words, no feeling anybody up just to make them scream, including Rosina Washington, no rages or any fist-banging on the dining room table, no remarks about the president and "all his stinking right-wing Republican shitheads," no Communist Party marching songs, no mawkish sobbing scenes about free love and utopia or any remembrances about my father and

Dr. Eshelman back in the old days when they went off together to fight in the Spanish Civil War, no discussion about the shrapnel still lodged in Dr. Eshelman's backside that itched so bad whenever it rained that it made him curse so savagely that no one could stand being in the same room with him—That night everything and everyone was on his tiptoe best.

That night the house was shined up to a sparkle. Window shades that had been brown and curly for years were replaced. Lamp shades that were burned and ragged on the inside were replaced. New crystal ashtrays were bought at the five-and-ten. My grandmother and Rosina Washington brought all the food to our house that night instead of having it at my grandmother's apartment, along with my grandmother's best sterling silver swan salt and pepper boats with the delicate blue glass cups, her old wine-stained Battenburg tablecloth wrapped in tissue paper that was only brought out for birthday parties, wedding anniversaries, the High Holy Days and Passover, along with the twenty-four matching wine-stained napkins that were pressed carefully as the air of expectancy began to mount.

∽∾

Mrs. Hornstien was wearing a dark green velvet dress and coat that night with a little green velvet hat, not a bit of makeup on her face, just those great bones, her big blue eyes, her long straight white hair and that dazzling smile that she knew made everyone adore her instantly, the triple strand of luminous yellow pearls she always wore, the man's Hamilton watch with the stretch metal band pushed high up on the sleeve of her dress and that certain presence she had, that certain largess that always swamped everything and everyone in the room.

In those early years when I first knew Mrs. Hornstien, it seemed to me then that here was a woman who stood completely on her own, needing nothing that was not already within herself, but I was still a child—too young to know that nobody stands completely on her own needing nothing that is not already within herself.

The doorbell rang at six o'clock sharp, exactly when it was supposed to ring, and in the following excitement of all the introductions and congratulations with everybody being overly joyful, a certain ingenuous happiness made its first appearance in my life.

But in all the insincere kisses, and in all the awkward hugging, still, a renewal of all the broken dreams and of every expectation blossomed again as two separate families merged in the front hall of my mother's house on Aberdale Road to forge a brand-new strain.

The gray mink coat was a big success. Everybody tried it on, all my aunts, my mother, my fake aunt Sylvia Eshelman, and Rosia Washington, even Albert put it over his shoulders and started strutting up and down the wide front hall of my mother's house like a model on the runway as everybody was trying to overcome their newness by making wisecracks and acting silly. Everyone, that is, except Albert's younger sister Doris Taxin, who was the thinnest person I had ever seen. So thin, in fact, that she looked like a human toothpick with long, thin brown hair, too much makeup, and legs that were so skinny I wondered how they held her up.

"My mother is not the kind of person I'd ever be friends with if she WEREN'T my mother, so why would I be friends with her just because she IS?" were almost the first words Doris said, almost the first instant her foot was in the door.

"Golda Hornstien is the BOSS LADY," Doris sneered as she pulled me into the powder room with her, "which in plain English means that either you do EXACTLY what Golda Hornstien tells you to do, EXACTLY how she tells you to do it, and EXACTLY when she tells you to, or else look out — Golda Hornstien will turn on you like nobody ever turned on you in your LIFE!

"My advice to you," Doris sneered out of her prison of bad feelings as she got up from the toilet, wiped herself, flushed, and then started pulling up her panty hose, "is to just 'yes' her to death if you know what's good for you. But you will," she said as she stared at me. "I can tell just by looking at you that you don't have any fight."

∽∽∽ "I do not believe in long engagements!" Mrs. Hornstien announced as she took a piece of pot roast.

"Why wait until the fat gets hard around the chicken — I say, eat the chicken while it's still sizzling and delicious," she beamed as she was helping herself next to a nice juicy chicken breast and then carefully selected a more well done piece for her husband with that honed, expert sense of knowing exactly which piece of chicken of all the pieces of chicken in the universe would be the perfect piece for him.

By the time I met the Hornstiens, Mrs. Hornstien was much more than Oscar Hornstien's wife. By then she was his mother, nurse, manager, employer, servant, and best friend, as well as his business partner, trustee of his vast wealth and his primary moral influence, and she wore each of these titles proudly with every move she made.

"When Daddy and I were courting," she said as she started putting the broccoli on his plate, "Daddy couldn't keep his hands to himself for even five full minutes," she said, as she grinned at her little husband, "and I don't think times have changed that much, at least I HOPE they haven't," she beamed as she winked at her little husband whose cheeks were flushing scarlet as he smiled.

"That's why I say we should have the wedding IMMEDIATELY!" she announced. "That way the children will be safely married and off to Europe by the end of October which is exactly when and exactly where my son has always wanted to spend his honeymoon — am I right son?" she said as she looked at Albert.

"Albert, do you remember?" she asked, as she automatically snatched the roll out of little Oscar Hornstien's hand and began buttering it for him, "how sore you were at your sister Doris for staying away only six weeks when she and Stanley were on their honeymoon? And do you remember?" she asked, "because I certainly do," she said as she handed the roll back to her husband all buttered and ready to eat, "how you said that someday you were going to take a whole year off so that you and whoever you'd marry would see the entire world?" She looked at him.

"Well, son," she said as she took the potato kugel spoon that Rosina Washington was holding out to her, "someday has come," she smiled as she winked at Albert.

"So Mrs. Fish," she said to my mother as she began eating, "how many ushers and how many bridesmaids and how many guests on your side are we talking about?" She asked as she put down her fork so she could take the gravy boat that Rosina was holding out to her.

"But wait!" she said. "Before we go another step! Have we discussed where we are going to have it? I don't want to intrude on your decision, of course, Mrs. Fish," she said as she looked at Albert, "but I would certainly prefer to have the wedding at our apartment the same way as I've had all our family's big events," she said as she stared my mother down for what seemed to me then like the longest second in history.

"You don't have to worry, Mrs. Fish," she said as she glared at my mother for another interminable moment, "my daughter Doris was married there, a number of my husband's nieces were married there, Gregor Rastapolska, who at the time was the con-ductor of the Leningrad Symphony Orchestra, married the great mezzo-soprano Tanyella Torcheska there and both our sons had their bar mitzvah luncheons there with over two hundred guests at each," she said. "So you see, you don't have to worry, Mrs. Fish," she said again as she kept glaring at my mother, "our apartment is NOT EXACTLY A SHACK," she said as she glanced for a moment at Albert—"Am I right son? I wouldn't exactly call our apartment a hovel—would you?" she asked sarcastically as she winked at Albert.

"Right again!" Albert answered. "The Boss Lady is always right. Anyone who's got half a brain knows that!" Albert smiled.

"I promise you you really don't have to worry, Mrs. Fish," Mrs. Hornstien said, completely oblivious to Albert's wisecrack, "we've entertained ROYALTY—The biggest names from all over the world have been wined and dined in that apartment and they've always RAVED," she smiled as she took some sliced brussels sprouts that were drenched in butter, then some cauliflower in a thick pink lobster sauce which was my favorite and finally a handsome serving of candied sweet potatoes nestling under a blanket of sumptuous, crisp, brown-baked marshmallows, first for herself and then exactly the same amount for her little husband.

"My daughter Doris is no beauty," she said as she

reached over for my grandmother's salt and pepper boats, "but in the wedding dress that Norman Norell designed for her you should have heard them gasp when she walked into the living room on Daddy's arm.

"The whole house was filled with white lilies, white orchids, and white gardenias that night," she said as she was putting another piece of pot roast on her husband's plate. "We tented the whole terrace in pearl white satin with lights strung everywhere and that wooden dance floor they put down on the terrace. Doris, do you remember how that imitation marble dance floor looked with all those hand-painted flowers and ribbons and cherubs and stars on it like the dance floor all by itself was a Botticelli MASTERPIECE!"

"And such gifts!" she said.

"Doris," she said, "do you remember how we had them all on display in the dining room? Do you remember the silver, Doris, all the Jensen you got and all the Black Star and Gorham and all the Tiffany like every store in New York City was having a FIRE SALE! Which reminds me, Albert," she smiled at her son as she helped herself to another roll, "I know how crazy you are about the Hotel Bristol in Paris, but I'd like to suggest this time that you stay at

54

the King George Sank the Fifth like Doris and Stanley did . . . ask Doris," she said. "Doris—am I right? Wasn't that the hotel where they serve breakfast out on a little balcony that overlooks the Seine River?" she asked as she zeroed in on her daughter Doris and then eyeballed her down which was Mrs. Hornstien's way of giving a silent order to say Yes!

"In my opinion, Albert," she said as she turned to her son, "the right way to start your lives off together is EXACTLY the way that Doris and Stanley started theirs," she said as she looked over at her son-in-law Stanley Taxin, who was staring at her through eyes that said that no passion anymore, no fight or even any resistance had passed between them in so long that by now, finally, he felt not only safe in the complacency of his defeat, but even a little smug.

"Thanks to our Daddy," she said, "Doris and Stanley had a magnificent honeymoon beginning in Paris at the King George Sank the Fifth, then they went to Rome where of course you'll stay at the Hassler like they did, the Royal Danielle in Venice, London at Claridge's and then down to the Riviera where of course you'll stay at the Carlton which was the hotel that your brother Benjamin loved so much—do you remember, Doris, how much he loved it there?

"Oh well," she sighed as she looked at Albert,

"those were good days weren't they children? Benjamin was your best man, wasn't he Doris . . . our beloved Benjamin . . . do you remember how beautiful he looked that night—like an angel," she said, her eyes filling with those same red tears that never spilled.

And then, as her lower lip began to quiver and her hands began shaking so badly that she had to put down her knife and fork—the great disconnecting barrier of grief that rendered her completely alone where she had neither husband nor son nor daughter, nor friend or fellow human being—her prison of grief once again that kept her locked to her son Benjamin forever.

And as I was watching this, as I've watched it happen so many times in the years that followed, I wondered then for the first time as I've wondered so often over all these years, why it was that nobody, not her son, nor her daughter, nor her husband, nor her son-in-law lifted a finger to help her. Why was it, I wondered, that no one moved an inch or stirred or said one word to try to comfort Mrs. Hornstien? She was suffering an understandable agony that was plain to everyone at the table, and yet everyone in her family sat perfectly still as they continued eating and simply allowed the suffering to tear around the room unleashed—and that included me. I did nothing either.

I didn't get up and go over to her or put my arms around her or hold her hand—Nothing! And for that I'm sorry to this day, but I was so young, too young then to know what to do or how to do it. All I could do was watch as they watched—as my grandparents and all my aunts and uncles and my brother Kal and the Eshelmans watched until it was my mother, a complete stranger to her, who got up, went over to her, put her arms around Mrs. Hornstien's shoulders, put her forehead on Mrs. Hornstien's cheek, and wept with her, saying nothing.

Not far from my mother's house was a park next to the railroad station where there were big old trees and wooden benches and a few statues scattered here and there, and in the middle of dinner I got up, went out into the hall, put on the old beaver coat my aunt Charlotte had passed down to me, and then slipped out on tiptoe to get some air.

I can still remember feeling that first hint of fall in the air that night.

There was a thin drizzle and it was windy so that the rain felt like little razor blades were slicing my face as I made my way across the street, around the corner and then into the park and in the black of night, with a freezing rain tearing at everything it touched like a temper tantrum, I sat down on a wooden bench next to a statue of a bear. . . . What's happening to me, I remember thinking. . . . What's going on?

I knew that in the world I came from marriage was expected of every decent girl. I knew that she was expected to win a man any way she could and then for the rest of her life she was expected to hold on to him—this prize of all prizes—against all odds and against every threat, until just holding on to him became her life.

I also knew the night the Hornstiens came to my mother's house on Aberdale Road for the first time, the night I experienced that first flash of ingenuous joy as everyone was greeting everyone in my mother's big front hall, I knew that they were all doing exactly what they were supposed to be doing and that what was happening was exactly what was supposed to be happening . . . Civilization was winning another round as it ground on, crushing as it went some enormous part of the human spirit that thrives on freedom and on solitude—and I also knew as I was sitting on the park bench in the freezing rain that there was no way to stop it. . . . It was as inevitable as death.

Worse than that, the moment our secret was out, the moment Albert "declared himself" to both our families, something changed. It was like a curtain dropped, or some big invisible wall came down out of nowhere to separate Albert from everything and everybody as if to say that now that I was in the bag, now that I was safely on the shelf along with all of his other acquisitions, he could go back to the rest of his life. He hadn't looked at me once that night, not a smile, not a wink, not a stare—Nothing! The urgency that was so enormous before was over, so over in fact that it was almost as if he didn't need me at all anymore, and if that was the case, if Albert didn't need me—then who was I?

If he didn't need me, then all I'd be would be a shadow or a toy or some kind of silly joke that went on a honeymoon with him to Paris, and then to Venice, and then to Rome and London and down to the Riviera until life became one long pointless vacation in one big fancy hotel after the next that would go on and on forever and ever and ever.

I wanted to get out of my mother's house almost as much as she wanted me out of there. Not that she ever came right out and said it, but recently she had made little jokes about "needing more closet space," which to me was the same as handing me my walking papers, and I knew too that once I left I could never come back.

On top of that, I remember thinking that from the middle of eleventh grade she made it clear to me that there would never be enough money to send me to college, not with student loans or tapping relatives or even doing housework on the side. Since my father's long illness and death left us penniless and over our heads in debt, college for me was as wild a dream as being a movie star or having long blond hair, which was what I was thinking as I was sitting on the park bench in the dreary night—which was what I was thinking as I got up, bundled my old beaver coat around me and started walking back toward the house. Which was what I was thinking as I hung up my old beaver coat in the closet in the hall, went back into the dining room, sat down again and looked over at Albert, who was still inside his wall of glass, eating.

Then I looked at my brother Kal. When I was little he sat on my face and farted, cut off all my bride doll's hair and stuck a safety pin in my arm so deep it bled, then he said that if I told he'd kill me and my mother. I never told, but not because he told me not to but because if I did, I knew somehow or other they'd blame me.

Then I looked over at Doris Taxin and her husband Stanley, polished with every hair in place, button-perfect people, foreign, walled off, Sanforized and all varnished up, whom I knew I would never be able to say a real word to as long as I lived, nor they to me.

That's what I was thinking as I looked next at

Mrs. Hornstien and at her little husband Oscar, utter strangers sticking up and out of place on this old familiar landscape I loved so well—who were these strange, funny-looking people sitting in my mother's house with all my aunts and uncles with my grandmother cutting the meat for my cousin Olympia Krantz with her one chromosome too many, her sand-colored hair, her too-pug nose and her too-round face who didn't know if she was a bird or a song or a poem or what as she sat smiling at Dr. Eshelman, my mother's lover, who I was in love with too since I was four or five years old, I was thinking as I looked at his big red face and his straight white hair and his fat red lips—good old Jack Eshelman, where would I have been without his big blustering goodness to me all my life. . . . Better not to mess around outside the house, I was thinking, because you go to where the passion is, as my gaze moved next to my mother, resplendent in her yellow satin lounging pajamas.

My mother, with her dyed pitch-black hair and her chalk-white skin sitting at the head of the table, smoking a cigarette and watching me as my eyes went around the room.

∽∾∾ "So," Harriet said at the breakfast table the following morning, "why so jumpy last night? What's going on with you?" she said, her face set in rock, her eyes not blinking as she glared at me. "What's going on, Marty?" she asked again as she stopped setting the table so she could glare at me even harder.

"I'm not going to marry Albert," I answered, quaking—I knew now beyond a doubt that she not only needed "more closet space" but that she needed me out of there in general. By now it was clear that Dr. Eshelman didn't come to visit me every afternoon, which was what she told me when I was younger. By now it was clear that I was not only an encumbrance to her but a big responsibility and an even bigger bother which I was genuinely sorry about, but nonetheless, I didn't want to get married. Not just yet. In the back of my mind, behind a lot of weights that felt like iron in my head, I had the wild idea—

the insane dream—that maybe someday, somehow, I could become a doctor, a painter, or simply go with my friend Turk Erving to Israel to farm the land. . . . I wanted to be free. That was all I wanted. All I wanted were a few months out of an entire lifetime to call my own. Albert Hornstien was a certainty, and at that moment more than anything under the sun I wanted the uncertainty that freedom is.

"Please, Mommy," I begged her, "let me go to college."

"WE DO NOT HAVE THE MONEY!" she answered.

"How about a student loan. I'll do housework. Anything—Please!"

"Marty," she said, "you don't let a thing like this go by. A man like Albert Hornstien, a family like the Hornstien family with that kind of MONEY! What are you? Out of your MIND?"

∽∾

As far back as I can remember, and for as long as I can remember, my mother was the one great overpowering love of my life.

To me she was far more than mere flesh and blood.

She was a kind of goddess, a kind of irresistible seductress who had snared me in her magical web from the first moment I opened my eyes, and from that first moment I was wild about her almost like I was in love with her the way a man would be.

Her hair was ink black and she had the whitest skin, but not just white, it had a translucence like alabaster. Her hazel eyes had heavy lids like the awnings on my grandmother's summer house in Atlantic City, and on top of that, the smell of her perfume as she'd bend over to kiss me mingling with the smells of her body, her breath and her crotch fascinated me. I used to lie in bed pretending to be sleeping, and while she was kissing me I was inhaling her like she was some kind of narcotic. The fact that she was very different than anyone I had ever known, and certainly different than any of my friend's mothers, wasn't apparent to me as a child. All I knew then was that I lived and breathed and waited just to be near her—anywhere, anytime, all the time.

That she used to like to grab fistfuls of candy from the wooden barrels at the five-and-dime or a pair of earrings on a little white paper card, a couple of lipsticks, and an eyebrow pencil, jam them into her pocket, grab me by the arm, and then tear out of there while she was assuring me as we were running that the five-and-dime could afford it better than we, made her more exciting than anyone I ever knew. Or the reason Dr. Eshelman was sitting on the sofa every afternoon when I came in from school, both of them drinking gin and gazing into each other's eyes, the reason he was there she said was because he wanted to see me "every day because he loved me so much" made me tear home from school as fast as I could run because I was wildly in love with Dr. Eshelman too, and like my mother, I also couldn't wait to be with him every afternoon.

Add to that the fact that she would never let me go to school if it was raining, snowing, or if it was icy out, and sometimes she wouldn't let me go simply because she wanted to go into town that day and have a little chicken chow mein, egg roll, and fried rice at Cathey Gardens Chinese Restaurant on Chestnut Street and she wanted company.

Cathey Gardens Chinese Restaurant had a band at lunchtime, so first we'd eat, then we'd fox-trot around the dance floor a couple of times—she would lead. Sometimes we'd pay and sometimes we'd dance out the door without paying depending on my mother's cash flow, and then for the rest of the afternoon we'd mosey hand in hand along Pine Street browsing the antique shops and kibitzing with the dealers with an eye out all the time for a beautiful

Majolica pot or a wonderful old Victorian rocker for the upstairs den.

To me all of this was wonderful and none of it was out of the ordinary. Not Dr. Eshelman, or stealing, or hooking school in order to go dancing with my mother, or sometimes just staying home from school to rub her feet because that day she was "very tired." It wasn't until I was in high school and had friends — one in particular, my best friend, Turk Erving, who told me how wacky all this was. "She's out of her MIND, Marty," Turk used to say, which used to make me furious because Turk didn't know any of the details so I'd clam up when she'd start talking because as I began to understand how different my mother was, her differentness from the beginning of my awareness of it didn't make me hate her the way Turk wanted me to, it made me sad.

Turk Erving was the Zionist daughter of two psychiatrists who were not only not Zionists, but ardent anti-God and antinationalist intellectuals whose only child was going to Jerusalem the following fall to Hebrew University. . . . "Jerusalem," she'd whisper across the darkness when she'd sleep over, "let's go the summer we graduate. God is sprawled on top of the Western Wall waiting for you to COME HOME, Marty," she'd say, "so when school is out," she'd say, "the minute after we graduate, let's just GO! We'll live on a kibbutz and work the fields for something that REALLY MATTERS—Not all this bullshit crap about which colleges you get into and what kind of clothes you're taking AND WHAT KIND OF HI-FI SET!

"Marty," she'd whisper across the darkness, "Israel is our reason for being ALIVE. This is our PURPOSE," she'd keep whispering. "Israel is about the HUMAN SPIRIT, Marty," she'd say. "It's about people who wouldn't be destroyed and that invincibility is the air you breathe and it's in the smell you smell and it's in the look on everybody's face—they look like TRIUMPH! Marty because they've come through and the best part," she'd whisper extra quietly, "over there," she'd say, "everyone screws with everyone all the time because it's all FREE LOVE! Everybody does it with anyone they want, and especially in the army. . . . Just IMAGINE such a thing. . . . Just IMAGINE IT. . . . And, Marty, over there," she'd say, "not only is there FREE LOVE with the cutest boys on the face of the EARTH, but over there a woman's the same as a man sexually. . . . Everyone's EQUAL! . . . Marty," she'd say, "this is our CHANCE!"

"My mother would die if I even mentioned it," I'd whisper.

"Your mother is insane, Marty. Anyone who won't let her daughter go on to college because she says she can't afford it, yet she wears a MINK COAT to the grocery store—Marty," she'd say, "OPEN YOUR EYES! Your mother's a selfish, self-centered MONSTER who my mother and my father BOTH SAY is what's known as a narcissistic borderline sociopath who doesn't care about anything except HERSELF! Anyone who holds her child back from going on to a school like THE UNIVERSITY OF PENNSYLVANIA when that child not only got in but is also willing to do housework just so she can stay there is a MONSTER and if she's a MONSTER, what do you care WHAT she thinks or says or DOES? Open your eyes, Marty, she doesn't give a HOOT IN HELL ABOUT YOU, if you want to know the truth. My parents BOTH SAID that all she cares about is HERSELF AND MONEY. . . . Marty, she said, "I'm going to Israel the minute school is over. I'm starting Hebrew University next fall, but over the summer," she said, "I'm going to work for my aunt who's a big shot in the government and she said she'd also give you a job that pays enough for you to live because you'd live with her AND GO TO SCHOOL because she can get you a FULL SCHOLARSHIP AT HEBREW UNIVERSITY because she knows EVERYBODY, and anyhow," she said, "anyone who could get into the University of Pennsylvania would qualify for all the financial help that's available at Hebrew University. Don't you SEE, Marty," she said, "it's your chance, so just think about it," Turk was begging me. "Think about the things I'm telling you," she'd say over and over, which was exactly what I was doing the next morning as my mother and I were standing on either side of the kitchen table glaring at each other.

"If we can't afford college next fall," I said, "then I'm going to Israel with Turk Erving this summer, and in the fall, if I come back, then we'll talk about getting married and about Albert and about the Hornstiens. But it's going to have to wait till I get back," I said. "My friend Turk Erving not only got me a job," I said, "but she got me a place to stay, which is with her aunt who's a big shot in the government," I said, quaking, because there I was, daring for once in my life to buck this woman who nobody ever dared to buck or to cross or to even argue with because she wasn't reasonable. Things were always the way my mother decided even if she was dead wrong because she was too crazy and too strong and I knew it. I might not have told my friend Turk Erving, but I knew it all. I knew more than she would ever know about this woman and I knew all the details like I also knew what made her the way she was, which didn't make it any easier for me. In fact it made it doubly hard because I understood my mother inside out.

"Turk Erving wants you to go with her to ISRAEL," she hissed, her eyes glaring even harder. "That little JERK—THAT LITTLE BUM! Those highbrow intellectual parents of hers, those two loony psychiatrists believe in FREE LOVE, Marty, so tell me, is that why you want to go to Israel with her? Well, is it Marty? I never liked that girl from the minute she put her foot in this house—who the hell does she think she is," my mother seethed, "that spoiled, self-centered, selfish kikey little pain in the ASS! I don't know who she thinks she is or where she thinks she's coming from to even DARE suggest a thing like ISRAEL to you," she roared at me across the china cups and saucers she stopped arranging for our breakfast.

"Marty? Are you CRAZY?" she said. "Albert Hornstien, who only comes from one of the biggest families in Philadelphia, has asked you to MARRY HIM and you are going TO MARRY HIM AS FAST AS YOU CAN before someone else gets her hands on him and—bom—just like that—the catch of the century will be GONE—do you UNDER-STAND?" she glared at me even harder.

71

"Marty," she said, "this man can give you every-thing under the sun. He is good-looking. He is swanky. He has millions of dollars and he comes from one of the best families in this city. His parents made an EMPIRE with their own two hands and they are going to give that empire to YOU lock, stock, and barrel! The Horn Cigar Company will be YOURS one day. How else, Marty, do you think you'll ever get ANYTHING IN THIS LIFE? Do you think, even in your wildest DREAMS, that you could ever EARN that kind of money in TEN LIFE-TIMES? Don't you know that all the girls who are going to the University of Pennsylvania come Sep-tember are looking for THEIR Albert Hornstien? Don't you think that every girl who is going to Israel this summer to work in a field is also looking for HER Albert Hornstien, and don't you think if they are lucky enough to nail one, they would nail him as fast as you could blink AN EYE!

"Maybe you don't love him right this minute because the only person you've ever loved in your entire life is ME," my mother said, "but I promise you that in fifteen years you will not only be MADLY IN LOVE WITH THIS MAN, but you'll also be madly in love with all the jewelry and all the fur coats and all the dresses he will pile on you, not to mention the houses and cars. Financial security is not something to sneer at, look at me," she said, "and look what's happened to us without it, I can't possibly send you to college now, but if you marry Albert Hornstien, the next ten generations of your family will all not only be able to go to college, but they WILL ALL BE ON EASY STREET living in the lap of LUXURY—tell me, Marty, is that SO TERRIBLE?" she glared at me.

We were standing at the kitchen table, she was leaning on it with both hands as she glared while I was standing limply in my pajama top across from her.

"Mommy, I'm going to Israel with Turkie Erving," I whispered, so shaken from the terror I felt for this woman that I could barely talk. "I already have a job," I said, "I already have a place to stay, it's only for the summer," I managed to lie as I looked her straight in the eye.

"Marty," she glared at me, her whole body leaning toward me—her eyes not blinking, "if it was anyone else," she said, "any lesser catch I'd say go on! who cares! do what you want! BUT THIS MAN IS THE CATCH OF A LIFETIME! Any girl in her right mind would DROP OUT OF ANY UNIVERSITY UNDER THE SUN in two seconds flat and come running back to Philadelphia from Israel in two more seconds flat to nab a man like ALBERT HORNSTIEN! Marry him, get a divorce, get a couple of million dollars in your pocket, and THEN GO TO ISRAEL WITH anyone you want, but at least that way you'll have a couple of dollars in your pocketbook, a few decent dresses in your suitcase, and a little fur coat. That way you won't be just another little NOBODY who doesn't have two nickels to her name and anyhow, where do you think you're going to get the money to even get there?"

"Turk said her parents would lend me the money, and since I have a job as well as a place to stay I'd be able to start paying them back right away."

"Oh, so you and Turk Erving have it all figured out—do you? I don't think you understand," she said very slowly like she was talking to a moron. "Money," she said, "is very important, more important than you can ever begin to even imagine. In fact," she said, "it's probably the only thing that matters in the END. If you don't believe me look at us," she said very slowly, like I didn't understand the English language. "We have to take in boarders to pay the mortgage since your father's death which left us PENNILESS AND OVER OUR HEADS IN DEBT! Is this what you want? Is this what you would like to have happen to you someday, or would you like maids and clothes and parties and naps when you're exhausted? But you need MONEY, Marty, and you don't have two NICKELS!"

"PLEASE, Mommy," I said as I swallowed down the tears, "PLEASE," I said again. "I want to go to Israel with Turk and work in the fields and live one summer on my own before I walk through those iron gates that will clang me closed inside once and for all."

"Marty," she said, "I've been around the block a few more times than you. I know what the story is. I know what I'm talking about and when I tell you that finally the only thing that isn't boring is money, you should LISTEN!" she said, still glaring at me while she was leaning on the kitchen table with both her hands.

"This man is not going to sit around twiddling his thumbs while you're off working in some field with TURK ERVING!" my mother said. "Believe me, a man like that will not be by himself for LONG! because some other girl who has a brain will have her claws in him before you can count to TEN! and then—bom—she'll take him to bed, do a couple of eights with her hips and THAT WILL BE THAT! No more Albert Hornstien.

"Marty," she said, "one day Turk Erving will become boring to you because one day all your girl-friends will become boring," she said, "husbands become boring, lovers become boring, sooner or later EVERYTHING BECOMES BORING EXCEPT

MONEY! Money does not get boring, Marty. In fact," she said, "the more you have, the less boring it becomes, and as for Israel," she said, "it's for KIKES! It's the kikiest place on EARTH — ICH!" my mother said as she continued glaring at me.

"Mommy," I said, "would you rather see me married or happy?" I asked.

"What's happy? You tell me what happy is. Right now you're feeling a little bit pressured which is making you say a lot of crazy things, but that's only natural because after all, you're only seventeen years old," she said as she kept glaring at me. "Before I married your father I asked my mother just like you're asking me what I was doing with my life.

"I was seventeen, too," she said, "and I was cute and fresh and full of hopes just like you are now and I remember just like you asking Grandma just like you're asking me what I was doing. It felt like my life was going right out the window, I told Grandma, and do you know what Grandma said? She said you're doing exactly the right thing, Harriet. Believe me, Grandma said, marriage is a good thing ONCE YOU GET USED TO IT! and I'm saying the same thing to you — marriage is a good thing, Marty, ONCE YOU GET USED TO IT, and in your case," she said, "you'll get used to it very fast because you are standing on the threshold of the most brilliant marriage of the century, the kind of marriage that nobody gets a chance at twice," she said, "so if God forbid you're dumb enough to toss Albert Hornstien back into the marketplace, mark my words, he'll be plucked up by the time you're on that plane to Israel by someone who understands the fact that marriage is marriage. It is NOT romance. It is NOT wild passionate love. It's a BUSINESS DEAL PLAIN AND SIMPLE, and in this case the deal is with a man who is a millionaire twenty times OVER, a man who is HANDSOME and SMART and comes from one of the best families in the entire CITY OF PHILA-DELPHIA, and you stand there telling me you want to go to Israel with some kikey little jerk to plant a GARDEN. . . .

"Marty," she said, "do you want to have to go to work every day of your life from nine to five, rain or shine, sick or well, and so exhausted sometimes that you can't stand up and then you come home dead tired, but before you can even sit down for a minute to catch your breath you have to clean the house, make dinner, clean up the dishes, do the wash, iron the clothes, and then maybe you can watch a little TV before you fall asleep snoring on the sofa," she said still glaring at me with both hands still on the kitchen table.

"Well," she said, "that's how ninety-nine-point-

nine percent of the whole world live their lives—
housewives, secretaries, nurses, doctors, lawyers,
and even Zionists in the Negev Desert in Israel, 'in
quiet desperation,' like someone said. Life is no pic-
nic! It's hard," she said. "Just look at me if you don't
believe me. And what makes it hard is one little
thing, NOT HAVING ENOUGH MONEY to relax
a little and have a couple of little luxuries.

"Marty," she said, "you are a radiant young beauty
who can have her pick of any man she wants. I never
had that opportunity. I had a big nose and my eyes
were too close together," she said still glaring at me
with both her hands still on the kitchen table. "But
you," she said, "are a gorgeous ripe young peach, and
Marty," she said, "you have to cash in on your youth
and on your beauty NOW," she said, "BEFORE IT
DISAPPEARS! because it's a saleable item—do you
understand?" she said as she glared at me.

Then my mother let out a long exasperated sigh,
straightened herself up, lit a cigarette, and walked
over to the stove to put the water on for tea.

∽∾ The wedding was held at the beginning of June at the Hornstiens' palace high over Rittenhouse Square.

My dress was designed by Norman Norell with a lace veil that went all the way to the floor even in front. The apartment that night was covered in white orchids, white gardenias, and white lilies that made the whole place smell like paradise, and as I stood at the top of that winding flight of white marble stairs beside my brother Kal, and as he put out his arm for me as the wedding march began, I remember thinking how I wished that flight of winding white marble stairs would go on and on and on and on and on and never stop.

Down the stairs, through the hall, into the living room, down the aisle between great iron candelabras that were draped in lace and flower streamers, to the enormous orange marble fireplace where Albert was waiting with the rabbi.

That night I flew in a plane for the first time, slept in a frilly nightgown that had a matching robe instead of my usual pajama tops for the first time, and in the dim light of the bridal suite of the King George "Sank the Fifth" Hotel in Paris, for the first time I witnessed a man having pleasure because of me. I remember the feel of his warm breath on my ear and the heat in his body as he was pressing mine and as he bucked and pounded in the dark, I remember looking at the ceiling and then at all the pictures on the walls and then at the windows and then at the white satin drapes pulled shut as I was thinking of all the things my mother told me like a broken record that was stuck and ticking in my mind. "Marriage," she said the day before the wedding, "is about SEX PURE AND SIMPLE, so in bed," she said, "you must always do everything and I mean EVERY-THING your husband wants, and what's more," she said, "you must always do it like you're thrilled, and even if you're not so thrilled," she said, "do it anyhow because from now on," she said, "pleasing your husband in bed will be the most important responsibility of your entire life. They do all the work," she said. "All you have to do is just lie there and moan like you're eating a nice juicy lamb chop and while you're moaning you can plan what you'll have for dinner that night or what you'll wear when you go out for lunch the next afternoon with the girls. . . .

"Next thing," she said, "NEVER and I mean NEVER say no to sex no matter how much you're not in the mood. Remember this, it's a very SMALL inconvenience for what you're getting back. Men want it all the time," she said, "which is what's so disgusting about them. It really bothers me how much like animals they are, but remember," she said, "if you say no to Albert Hornstien, there will ALWAYS be someone right behind you who will be more than willing to say yes to him in one second flat, and then—bom—just like that, someone with an eye out to snatch him away from you before you can say jackrabbit will have her claws into him, but by the same token," she said, "and this is very important, NEVER! and I mean NEVER! let him feel too comfortable with you. Let him always think that you have one foot out the door yourself because— and now I'm going to let you in on something—the whole secret to passion where it comes to men is INSECURITY!

"The minute a man gets too comfortable," she said, "the instant he takes his shoes off mentally—bom— someone will come along, someone who knows a few tricks about how to keep him dangling a little and always a little bit on the edge, someone whose mother told her that she has to make the number eight with her hips while she's screwing him which of course drives men completely out of their MINDS, and if she can make him feel a little bit unsure of her and if she does her number eights real good — bom — right out the door like he never EVEN KNEW YOUR NAME!

"Men live by their juniors, Marty," she said, "because that's what they think love is, remember that! and remember too that the LAST THING IN THE WORLD THEY WANT IS PEACE, so the two main things for you to keep in mind," she said, as she got up to get another cigarette, "is that you have to keep him guessing all the time and you have to do your number eights real good and slow while you're screwing him.

"On top of that," she said, "always wash your business out with salt water to get that stink away, never be able to open a jar or a bottle because he should never think you're strong, never act like you have a brain because a brain on a woman is the kiss of death, dumb like a fox," she said, "that's the trick you have to cultivate, and finally," she said, "you have to start stealing from the household money every week. Do it this way," she said, "put half the money he gives you for the household into your stocking box and then give half of whatever you put in there to me," she said, as she glared at me, "because," she said, "this is the way women manage. This is what women have to do. It's the ones who don't do this who are the idiots," she said, "because how else does a woman expect to get a little edge in a world where money is EVERYTHING!

"Suppose," she said, "one day you want a little something and he doesn't want to buy it for you? If you have a couple of dollars tucked away in your stocking box you never have to even ask him. All you have to do is just go out and buy it, and this is also the way that women take care of their mothers which of course all good daughters do," she said, "without ever having to tell their husbands a single thing because after all," she said, "why should you be running around in minks and satin underwear while I'm in rags," she asked with a gray frozen look on her face that I'll never forget as long as I'm alive.

I remember I was staring at her the whole time she was speaking. I was sitting on the sofa in the upstairs den and she was sort of hovering above me in the fading light of late afternoon. No lamps had been turned on so I could barely make out her features as I was staring at her. She seemed that afternoon—this woman who was saying all those things—like a strange gray piece of rock that had somehow sprung up from the floor of the upstairs den like a statue made of granite. Was this really my mother talking? Could it be that this was who Harriet really was? And as I looked at her in the fading light everything about her looked strangely distorted. Her nose, which was the first nose job in Philadelphia, this nose that she was so enormously fond of, seemed to have shrunk along with all the puffed-up courage she had to have to have such revolutionary surgery solely for the sake of vanity. But vanity to Harriet Fish was the great taproot that hooked a person into survival and survival was what my mother worshiped—this predatory little bird who demanded and needed and wanted EVERYTHING!

My mother always had the best. Designer dresses by the closetsful and fabulous evening gowns and real alligator pocketbooks and high-heeled shoes in every color, and that was not to even mention two mink coats and all her pins and bracelets and earrings and necklaces that first my father provided her with and when he died it fell to my brother Kal as a kind of privilege to keep the presents coming. She had a knack, Harriet Fish, for turning everyone she knew into her slave, and that was especially true for my brother Kal and me because we loved her only she didn't know we loved her, that was the saddest part, she couldn't imagine how anyone could love her or why, and so we always had it over our heads to prove it to her and no one ever could.

"Start out by sending me four hundred dollars a month," she said. "That won't break any of them, I can assure you, because it only comes to one hundred dollars a week which anyone with any intelligence can very easily siphon off the top of her household cash without her husband ever suspecting a thing. With all their money," she said, "this will be like two little grains of sand taken off the whole Atlantic and the whole Pacific beaches put together, while for me," she said, "it will be a new mink hat or maybe a stunning new pink cashmere cardigan. Then," she said, "when you're a little more deeply entrenched into their family, after you've burrowed yourself more securely into your own little niche, then you can up it little by little until you hit three or four thousand dollars a month, which they'll never miss, I promise you, not with the kind of money those people have, whereas for me, it will be a cushion against my becoming ragged and shabby as I'm getting older," she said, as she stared at me like her eyes had become two desperate contracts I had to sign.

Paris was the first stop. Then Berlin, Venice, and then down to the Riviera where we stayed at the Carlton Hotel for over seven weeks because that's where Benjamin stayed and shopped and ate and walked. Our little pilgrimage. Our deep respects.

"On second thought, don't have children," Mrs. Hornstien whispered to me at the rehearsal dinner the night before the wedding. She took me aside, visibly shaken by all the toasts and all the celebrating, and as she put her hand on mine she said, "God is hard on mothers—too hard," she whispered, "if you don't lose them to death, then you lose them to life, which I promise you will break your heart. It's their childhood," she said as her eyes welled up with those big red tears that never spilled. "Those precious years when you're their entire world and they're your every thought—How are you ever supposed to get past a thing like that?" she asked as she looked at me. "Their childhoods are the most precious years of a woman's life—they're the biggest thrill there is on earth—bigger," she said, "than all the fame and fortune and all the cars and boats and jewels and houses on EARTH. Tonight how much I wish I could have those sweet years back," she whispered, "because maybe if I could, maybe somehow I'd know how to do a better job. We were all only amateurs," she said as she clutched my hand, "and that's the tragedy, that we were all amateurs when it comes to raising children. We made mistakes. We did so many things that were impatient and unkind and insensitive. But Marty," she said, "we were also only HUMAN," she said as her lower lip began contorting in pain. "We come to parenthood with our own limitations, our own weaknesses, our own needs and fears," she said, "but we come with an honest heart to do the best we can with THEIR BEST INTEREST AT THE CORE OF EVERYTHING, but now," she said, "I'll never have the chance to make up to him for how I may have hurt him as he was growing up. It's too late," she said. "Tomorrow he's getting married which means it's all over between my son and me which is why a wedding is just another kind of shivah," she said as her eyes filled up again with those same red tears that never spilled.

∾∾∽

In those days I used to look at Mrs. Hornstien and wonder what in God's name was she talking about.

Was this just the babbling of an old woman or was

she making sense. But I was so young then, too young to even have a clue about what she was talking about so what could I say—how could I possibly answer, she always talked like that to me and I never knew what to answer, not ever.

On the Riviera when we were at the place where Benjamin was killed, I asked Albert if he missed his mother as much as I missed mine, and he said no. In fact, he said he never even thought about her. And when I asked him what he thought about her life and how she lived it and how she struggled with her pain, he told me he never stopped to think about his mother, or her pain, or how she lived her life. "My mother never talked to me about herself," Albert said. And then Albert said that when he met me he fell in love almost the first instant he laid eyes on me. "I was driven beyond myself," Albert said.

"I was like a bee flying over a flower that had a lot of honey. I felt like a homing pigeon who homed right in. . . . I had no control," he said, "which never happened to me before, and then," Albert said, "when you smiled, your smile and your teeth—why your teeth I don't know—but there was something about your teeth, something that stupid sealed me forever and that was IT! I was cooked! I guess it happens once in a lifetime," Albert said. "I guess it's the passion that glues you to that person, but THAT's what I think about—the passion, your teeth, how glued I am to you," Albert said, "not my MOTHER!"

On the ship coming home from our honeymoon I told Albert about the money my mother was asking for.

I told him it felt like she was holding me up with a gun and even though it was true, I said, that my father left us penniless and over our heads in debt, and even though my brother Kal was doing the best he could to provide for her, still, in spite of all my brother's efforts and in spite of all the bills and debts, she had longings for things like a little mink hat or a new pink cashmere sweater and that was why she put the squeeze not only on me but also on all my uncles, and it wasn't just my uncles, either—she was demanding large sums of money from half a dozen people in the neighborhood whom she said it was perfectly okay to "approach" because they "all were loaded" and since they "all were loaded!" she said she wasn't going to kill herself either trying to pay them back because according to her it wouldn't make or break them anyhow.

On top of that, I told Albert, she was trying to get some money out of a few of my father's wealthy patients whom she believed owed us a little something "extra" because my father saved their lives which made her feel entitled to whatever she could finagle out of them, same as she was all but blackmailing a few old friends of hers who once made the sad mistake of divulging things to her they never should have uttered to a living soul, but since they did, now they'd have to pay. She never put it that way exactly, but she did tell me in a very excited tone of voice that "the prospects for some new cash looked suddenly very promising."

The real problem, I told Albert, was that Harriet felt absolutely entitled to anything under the sun, no questions asked, and it didn't matter either if what she felt entitled to belonged to someone or to ten thousand people—if she wanted it that was it, and worse, if she didn't get what she wanted when she wanted it she'd go into a rage, which was why the night his family came to dinner I was a wreck because I knew that one wrong word or one wrong gesture, especially from his mother, even though Harriet appeared to be extremely elegant in her yellow satin lounging pajamas with the golden threads and the tiny seed pearls on the pockets, and even though the family Sheffield platters with the copper coming through were all cleaned up and shining, with all the flowers that night and the candles and the lace tablecloth that belonged to my grandmother, resplendent with all its little holes and wine stains, and even the odd collections of silverware and dishes from all the different sets of dishes and silverware that had survived since my great-great grandmother, with my mother presiding over everything like a calm, normal person who could prepare chicken cacciatore on a bed of rice like it was no big deal, and even though my aunt Olivia Krantz didn't wear her black fishnet stockings that night with her red hightop sneakers or her fake leopard turban, and my brother Kal didn't ask my cousin Olympia Krantz with her too-round face and her too-pug nose and her little funny eyes because of her one chromosome too many to sing "Over the Rainbow," and even though all my uncles talked to everyone that night with big fake smiles on their faces—in spite of all of this, I knew we were still all sitting on a keg of dynamite because one wrong word from his mother, or even one wrong look and Harriet would have gone at her like a rabid animal. And what was more, I told him, she said she had "her fingers crossed" that I would one day be able to come up with "something a little bit more substantial" in the way of cash, and then I told him that from the moment she leveled all of this at me the day before the wedding until the moment I was telling it all to him, it caused me so much sorrow that my honeymoon was torture.

Then, without a moment's hesitation, Albert told me that I was to give her exactly what she wanted and I was to give it to her exactly the way she wanted it. He told me to give her four hundred dollars a month to begin with as if I were stealing it directly out of his trouser pockets every night and then he said when we got back he would take care of the debts and burdens my father's illness had incurred, but, he said, only on the condition that I begin wearing the diamond ring I had been afraid to show her, and as I nodded in agreement, it began to dawn on me how magnificent, enormous, and touching it is — this thing that goes on between a husband and a wife.

Part II

ᘒ Where could he be, I'm wondering as I look at my watch again. Over an hour late and still no call which is not at all like Albert who has become even more dependable, even more reliable and considerate, than he was even then.

Maybe, I'm thinking as I glance at my watch, I was wrong about the time we said we'd meet—or maybe, which is more likely, what might have happened is that Albert ran into his brother-in-law Stanley Taxin on the way out of the office and the two of them stopped off at the club to have a bite. But then I'm thinking, what could have happened to Mrs. Keenan from Keenan Real Estate who was also supposed to be here along with the people who've bought the apartment.

And as I look for maybe the last time at this old familiar room, this now empty library of the Hornstiens' palace high over Rittenhouse Square, my eyes fill up. . . .

The windows are stripped and all the furniture is gone except for what's been saved for the auction block, and as I look at the bare wood floors without any of Mrs. Hornstien's Chinese rugs, a feeling of inestimable loss sweeps over me. It was in this room, as I look for the last time at the deeply vaulted ceiling with the whole zodiac carved into it, that I met Albert's mother over thirty-five years ago, this room with the mahogany bookcase walls and stained-glass windows where the family formed a receiving line to greet over three hundred guests at our wedding— how they all stood up when I walked in on the arm of my brother Kal, and how their low voices and the rustling of the ladies' taffeta gowns seemed so amplified then, like they were the whispered admonitions of a thousand generations all contained in this one room.

This room where our daughter Nancy, the oldest of our three children, took her first wobbly steps with her little arms up high as she came laughing toward us from Mrs. Hornstien's open arms—this room where our daughter Ruthie sang for her grandmother one Sunday afternoon and how suddenly all of us who were sitting here that day knew the kind of gift she had, and it was in here that our son Benjamin, the youngest, read his first word—S, he said, then T, then O, then P . . . STOP! he said carefully and full of hesitation. Then he said STOP, and then at the top of his lungs he shouted S T O P as we all started cheering and applauding, all of us firsthand witnesses to the miraculous wonder of the mind.

Benjamin riding the new three-wheeler that Mrs. Hornstien gave him up and down the whole length of the now empty hall with an Indian headdress on and a bow and arrow strapped to his back. Mrs. Hornstien was right when she said no one would have ever guessed that their childhoods would be the biggest thrill of all. Bigger, she said, than all the fame and fortune, all the cars and houses and jewelry or anything we could have ever imagined. We were all movie stars then, and the president of the world as we sat at the top of the highest mountain with our laughing children next to us, I'm thinking as I walk into the now empty living room with the gray stucco walls and the thirty-five-foot painted ceiling brought over for the Hornstiens from Austria.

This room, I'm thinking, as I lean up against the enormous orange marble fireplace where Albert and I were married, and then two years later in front of this same fireplace my brother Kal married Albert's gorgeous red-headed cousin Rosanna Keiser, and then a month after that we sat shivah in this room for little

Oscar Hornstien who at the end had gotten so white and flat against the sheets that all you could see were his green silk pajamas from Rudolphs in New York with his gold initials on the pocket, everything he owned came from Rudolphs, every pair of silk underpants, every shirt, every handkerchief. "Golda," he said toward the end, "there are no happy endings."

"Oh yes there are," she answered. "I'm right here with you, feeding you and kissing you and holding your hand like I've been holding it for over fifty-seven years. I can't cure cancer," she said, "or stop death but we're together and I'm here with you through everything, so wouldn't you consider that a happy ending? Oscar," she said, "do you remember that big black Packard? Remember, Oscar, it was the first car we owned before either of us could even drive it but we drove it anyhow all the way down to Atlantic City with all our precious treasure in the back, and do you remember, Oscar?" she said as she kissed his forehead, "how the policeman gave us a ticket for going too slow on the White Horse Pike—or, Oscar, was it the Black Horse Pike? I don't remember which," she said, "like I can't remember the address of that freezing fourth-floor walk-up behind the Girard Trust Bank—do you remember Oscar," she said, "how we had to bundle up to roll those cigars with the mufflers and the hats and the coats and the gloves and steam was still coming out of our mouths, that's how cold it was up there," she said as she kissed his hand which she was holding and stroking. "How many pair of gloves did we wear at a time — three? four? We were so young," she said, "that we could do anything — am I right?" she said. "We didn't have two nickels to our name but we had each other didn't we, Oscar, and that's all we needed, wasn't it? Just each other," she said as she kept kissing his hand and stroking his forehead.

"Oscar," she said, "do you remember how we used to take the children to the movies every Saturday afternoon, rain or shine, and how they always fought to sit next to you, I was always on one side so we could hold hands just like I'm holding your hand right now, and only one of them got to sit on the other side, and the way they would fight and kick and push each other to get next to you — do you remember?" she said as she bent over to kiss his smiling lips and then his forehead, "do you remember Oscar," she said . . . "Oscar . . . " she said again . . . "Oscar . . . " but this time he didn't answer. Not ever again. Then, three months later we sat shivah in this room again for our daughter Nancy, who died of leukemia with only five swift years tucked under her belt.

And as I walk back into the hall, empty now of all the paintings and pieces of thick black sculpture, gone to all their respective heirs — to Albert and to Doris and to the grandchildren along with all the rugs and furniture and crystal and china and all the books, I can almost see them coming down the stairs again together, immaculate natty Oscar Hornstien holding Nancy's hand, her fast little steps pulling him as he grinned. After the children leave home, Mrs. Hornstien used to say, no matter what you do, the whole place gets a musty mildew smell, especially in their bedrooms which become such unbearably desolate shells that even the sunlight in there turns to a kind of brown, lifeless haze. . . .

In the end, Mrs. Hornstien's beautiful bedroom on the second floor, with all the sunlight that used to fall in big broad bands of dusty gold across the tan satin bed with all the lace and satin, was reduced to a dimmed, drapes-drawn hospital room with nurses around the clock, vials of medicines, a commode, a walker, a wheelchair, and me.

In the end I was the only one who came to talk to her and read to her and comb her hair and I was the one who listened and listened and listened and listened and when I couldn't listen anymore I listened, while her own children would politely shut her up or start fidgeting or they'd just get up and leave while she was talking. "Oh no," she'd smile from deep inside her satin pillows on one of those long winter afternoons when it was just the two of us as it got to be more and more, when no one else was there which became more and more the case as her heart condition worsened, "don't tell me my daughter Doris loves me," she'd tell me as I'd sit in the chair beside her bed knitting, "she must HATE me if you want to know what my opinion is . . . too bad!" she said, "to have it end this way. There used to be a closeness," Mrs. Hornstien said, "she used to tell me things and include me and let me get a real foothold in her life, but that ended long ago. Once her daughter Leslie was born," Mrs. Hornstien said, "our relationship was never the same, it was as if the love she had for me went directly to her child like I didn't even exist anymore! And what a brat that Leslie is, what a little mess just like my daughter Doris, plus," she said, "after Doris went into therapy she started accusing me of everything that went wrong in her life until finally after a couple of years we drifted so far apart we were like two complete strangers who had nothing to say to each other anymore, and now," she said, "she hardly ever calls or comes or cares, and frankly," she said, "I'm just as happy with it this way because frankly I stopped caring myself which is eventually what happens which is why I say that if she didn't hate me, don't you think she'd come once in a while to see how the old girl's getting along? Marty," she said, "it's very simple, you love people who are good to you and you stop loving people who aren't good to you, which is why I've become more attached to you than I am to my own daughter. . . . I don't say I love you more but I love you as MUCH!" she'd say, "and why? because you've been a very good and loving child to me so how could I NOT love you. There are a few simple rules in life," she said, "if someone is good to you and is caring and kind and if that person LIKES you . . . I don't say LOVES . . . I say LIKES you, then," she said, "you have no choice but to eventually LOVE them back, want to or not! And by the same token," she said, "how can you continue to love someone who is uncaring, disinterested, and hurtful? You can't! It's impossible, even if that person happens to be your very own CHILD! Because even your own child, this human being who you'd lay your life down for in one second without thinking twice, can hurt you so much that you can absolutely stop loving her because it's a matter of survival, and survival," she said, "is the first rule of life.

"When you're a child," she'd say, "you need your

mother, and when you're a mother," she'd say, "you need your child, except when they grow up they don't need you! Oh," she said," they need your MONEY all right! No matter how much they have of their own, never mind, they want yours, too, every nickel of it, but not the old bundle who comes with it.

"Don't they think I know what they're up to, Marty?" she'd smile. "Don't they think I can read them like a book? They'll have to get up pretty early in the morning to pull one over on Golda Hornstien," she'd say, "so my advice to you," she said, "is don't chase after them as they get older, let them chase after you. It's better that way," she'd say. "It's more honest, and if we're talking about 'honest,'" she said, "my daughter Doris Taxin told me she'd never forgive me for making a 'slave out of her.' She told me I ruined her life because she only married Stanley Taxin 'to get away from me,' that bargain, Stanley Taxin, what an IDIOT my daughter is, I hate to say it but my own daughter Doris is an IDIOT! And while we're also speaking of idiots," Mrs. Hornstien said, "do you think I can ever 'forgive' her for the way she LOOKS! She looks like a concentration camp survivor who ought to just shut up and eat something once in a while instead of picking around at a little radish and calling that DINNER! From the time she was twelve years old," Mrs. Hornstien said, "she'd just sit there and not eat one single bite until I was pulling out all my hair and it never stopped, nothing but aggravation from the time she was that little girl who stopped eating until now when I'm bedridden with a serious heart ailment and she has to tell me, my brilliant daughter, that her whole life was always centered around me because that's the way I EXPECTED it. Then she told me after she went into therapy that I never 'let go of her for which she will never forgive me,' she said, and that's the reason why she 'HATES ME.' She said she even gave Leslie to me—her first child 'sacrificed,' she said 'at the altar of Golda Hornstien,' who by the way she wouldn't name for my mother like I asked her to because she said it's 'a criminal act to name a child after the dead,' because she said that's how you get 'destroyed by tradition,' and then she said, and this was the last straw, the trouble is, she told me, that she 'can't stay away from me no matter how much she HATES me'—I'm a 'MONSTER,' she told me, but even though she knows I'm a 'MONSTER,' she said she still can't stay away from me because I could never let go of her so she could never let go of me because I didn't teach her how to do it, she says, but she's working on it 'before it's too late,' she has the gall to say to me, so now she says she only comes because she has to, she only calls because she has to and she wants me to know it's all done 'grudgingly' and then she says, this idiot daughter of mine, that she absolutely had to tell me all of this or else her psychiatrist told her that 'anger held in turns to FAT'!

"I gave her life," Mrs. Hornstien said, "the best education—first she went to the Baldwin School, then she went to Wellesley with not just any interior decorator to do her room, but Bennett and Judith Weinstock Interiors who did the window treatments, the chair, the sofa, and her bedspread, who you can only fault for their addiction to the impeccable!" Mrs. Hornstien said, "and she went with the most gorgeous wardrobe, jewelry like you never saw, cultured pearls, little gold earrings from Cartier—anything she wanted, all the love in the world, the best care anyone could give another person and maybe twenty or thirty million dollars by then in cold hard CASH—In my opinion this is NOT A MONSTER!

"Once upon a time," Mrs. Hornstien said, "if a child would have dared talk to me that way I would have destroyed that child and then I would have been destroyed, but no more!" she said. "If she says I'm a monster, if she doesn't want to come, if she doesn't call, if she doesn't want to see me—then don't come, don't call, and don't see me because what's happened is that my feelings FOR HER have CHANGED! Now I don't want to see HER! and it's not a matter of not wanting to forgive my child. . . . I can't! Because she hurt me too much — a child can do that to a parent the same as a parent can do that to a child and then that's that! Something very big is finished that's never the same again.

"What my daughter Doris Taxin didn't understand wasn't that I wanted to 'make a slave out of her,' what I've always believed is that the family is a power unit," Mrs. Hornstien would say as I sat there knitting those long hours away. "I believed," she'd say, "that all the wealth and strength and assets had to be consolidated for all of us because no one on the outside gives a hoot in hell if we live or die. In fact," she'd say, "they would love to see us BLEED! But," she'd say, "I used to believe that if you have your family behind you — their support, their love, their strength and money — then you can get through anything, including even old age! That's what I used to think," she said, "but now that I'm older and wiser I'm thinking who knows? Maybe that's not the whole story either.

"There's an old saying that 'parents and teachers are people to be outgrown,' and if that's the case," she said, "then maybe a better gift to give your children and your grandchildren is not thirty or forty million dollars, but do like the gentiles do—let go of them and if they come back they come back, and if they don't, they don't," she said, with that certain wistful look she used to get whenever she was pondering the truly enormous issues that women face.

She was the real teacher of my life, the one I learned everything from, starting with not putting cold cream on my face before I went to bed—instead she told me to put on eye makeup, I'm thinking as I walk into the once most splendid dining room I'd ever seen in my life, empty now of everything except the gray satin walls and the gray satin ceiling, the gray satin drapes dripping with gray satin tassels, and braid and little silvery balls like Christmas ornaments and her enormous crystal chandelier wrapped in gauze and hanging from the ceiling like the victim of some incredible misfortune.

Mrs. Hornstien used to say that women died at least four times. Once when the children leave, once when they lose their looks, once when they lose their husbands, and once again when they can't go into their own dining rooms for dinner anymore, I'm remembering as I look around the shell of what was once such regal splendor. Gone, all the elaborate dinners Mrs. Hornstien used to give with gold lay plates, gold knives and forks, and Crump in his starched white jacket and Etta who did the cooking and Anna and Margaret and such exquisite food that Albert used to walk away from the table saying the food was so good he could go straight to the electric chair. Albert was always so much bigger than life to me, no trace of weakness, no human frailties, happy, big-spirited — generous — this man whose heart I've slept beside for over thirty-five years, I'm thinking as I glance at my watch again, he's gotten old too, like a worn bridge that everything has crossed — dogs, carts, horses, people. I chose to be safe, secure, and protected while all the time I longed agonizingly for everything exciting and wild which is how life breaks your heart . . . those dreams of freedom while I clung to the garden gate that clanged me safe inside the garden walls as though safety were an instinct I couldn't fight. Mrs. Hornstien was right when she changed her tune toward the end and said that finally, better than all the money in the world, is probably to do like the gentiles and just to let go of them, husbands and children, and if they come back, they come back, and if they don't, they don't, but in either case you've given the most there is to give another person — their freedom, guiltlessly and without strings.

In those early years I would listen to her talking with a sense of bored complacency knowing nothing then and yet expecting everything because my children were still small and I was still the center of their universe, I'm remembering as I'm staring at the big black concert grand piano that for some reason has been moved for now into the empty dining room, and as I walk over to it, to this old Steinway Mrs. Hornstien used to play with our daughter Ruthie sitting next to her on the bench, a young girl then with a voice of such unimaginable beauty that tears would always come to my and to Mrs. Hornstien's eyes every time Ruthie would start to sing. It was at this piano—this big old Steinway grand—that our then soon to be son-in-law Richard, the youngest of Ronnie Turner's five remarkable sons, asked Albert if he could have the "high honor of marrying our daughter Ruthie," because, Richard said, they were so happy when they were together that according to some law written in the clouds he knew they should be together forever and ever and ever and ever and ever. I don't remember being either happy or not happy when Albert asked me to marry him but when Richard asked us for our daughter Ruthie I experienced a kind of happiness I never knew I was capable of. The children were always the whole story for me—astonishing what depths they touch, but even still, I was tortured my whole life wondering what it would have been like if I had had the guts to have gone off to Israel with my friend Turk Erving when I was seventeen years old to build a dream. The chance was in my hands—all I had to do was to do it, and that chance, like a big breathing ghost, still sits on my shoulder, this big weight I still can't shake to this very instant, right now, this minute. What would it have been like to have reached for the stars, young and free, imagine the lovers, the idealists, the artists and writers who lived and worked and talked about a cause that was bigger than themselves. . . . Or what if I had gone on to the university and become a doctor—what a dream, what a life I might have had. "But there are no 'what ifs,'" Mrs. Hornstien used to say, "what if my grandfather were my grandmother, what if my horse were my dog. . . ." "So what in your opinion is the most important life a person can live?" I asked her once, on one of those long afternoons when finally she didn't get out of bed anymore, and without a moment's hesitation, without even the smallest break, as though she were waiting for this question all her life, she said, "it's all the same, it doesn't matter, none of that makes any difference, all that matters," she said, "is to have compassion—real compassion—it isn't easy," she said, "but if you have that, then you've accomplished everything," she said from so deep inside her satin pillows that by then it looked almost like nobody was there. . . . "In other words," I said as I kept knitting, "you don't really have to be anything. . . ." "No," she said "you just have to be kind—or let me put it another way," she said, "the worst thing you can do is to cause suffering to any living thing," and as I glance at my watch again I'm thinking how much I wish she were here now so I could just say thank you because I never really did, I'm thinking as I hear the front door bang and Albert's voice calling, "Marty, where are you, are you in the dining room?

"As I suspected," he says as he comes bounding in all smiles, big and red and happy. "Where have you been?" he says as he looks at me like he always does, with so much tenderness.

"Right here," I say. "Wasn't this where I was supposed to be?"

"No," he says. "You were supposed to meet me at Joanne Keenan's office while I signed the papers and got the check," he says, as he waves a big manila envelope in my face.

"How many years since the Boss Lady's gone. How many years since this place has been on the market without a single bite, and then," he says, "two million seven hundred and fifty thousand dollars in cold hard cash.

"Tell me, Marty," he says, "is that why you weren't at Joanne Keenan's office? Because you didn't want to see the old girl finally sold? What would we have done with all this space?" he asks as if he can read my mind. "Seven bedrooms," he says, "three maid's rooms, two terraces, each the size of half a tennis court, an upstairs den, a downstairs library, a living room, a dining room, halls, kitchens, pantries, a bar, seven bathrooms — but I knew it would come to this, that you'd be the one, not I, who couldn't face selling it. Why, Marty," he asks, "has this been so much harder on you than on me or Doris?" he asks, as he puts his hand on my back . . . and as I look at him standing next to our son Ben, and then as I look at Ben for a moment, I see in my son the young Albert of so many years ago — the same black curly hair, the same princely ankles, the same brown alligator loafers with the tassels, and the same sweetness, and as I stare at the two of them I wonder where it all went — all those flying years. . . . The old Bellevue Stratford Hotel, I'm remembering as I look over at Benjamin again. Mrs. Hornstien used to take a room every year so that all the grandchildren and all their friends could watch from the window the great plumed men all in their feathers and spangles playing their banjos as they'd strut up Broad Street on New Year's Day—it seems like it was only a strange yesterday ago with Mrs. Hornstien sitting on the sofa of that hotel room with Benjamin on her lap as she sang to him and rocked him in her arms. She was still so beautiful, with the bluest eyes and her long straight white hair and those bones and that nose and smile that was so dazzling it swamped everything and everybody when she flashed it with Benjamin on her lap who was such a little boy, all round, no bones, just his rosy flesh and laughing. It took a lifetime to realize what these people meant to me. I was so young then, too young to understand how much she gave and that nobody ever said a word of thanks, nobody ever put into words a hint of appreciation, in the end no one even listened to her, no one fussed or tended or bothered except a grudgingly dutiful daughter-in-law who didn't have a clue what an enormous gift this woman was.

A maid and a nurse. That's who was there at the end—the three of us—duty bound, impersonal and waiting to finally get it over with. . . . It takes a lifetime to learn about life, I'm thinking as my son Benjamin comes over to me. . . . I was too young then to realize that Mrs. Hornstien was more than just a shadowy beast that loomed almost unreal on the doorstep of my life. . . . Someone to be gotten rid of, pushed aside—conquered. She was Albert's mother so I never quite knew how to get past a kind of awkward strangeness, I could never quite achieve the kind of intimacy she longed for, this big woman, oldish even thirty-five years ago, whose foot was the first foot Albert ever kissed, hers were the first breasts he ever suckled, she was the first person he ever wrapped his small little arms around, and who she was and what she must have felt like wrapped itself back like concrete around his heart forever.

"Albert," I say as I clutch my son Benjamin's hand, "why didn't anyone ever mourn your mother when she died, or mourn her now as we're about to leave the home she created with so much love—why?" I ask him, "why was she so completely alone at the end?"

Albert quiet for a minute—thinking, then he says simply and clearly, the way he says everything, "We didn't need her anymore.

"No one needed her. In the end she was the one who was needy, but no one needed her. I guess you could even say that we were glad by then to finally be rid of her," he says. "Not that we were glad"—he quickly backtracks out of a flash feeling of instant guilt—"but," he says, "we had her in us so it didn't matter to us anymore if she died or not because we had her," he says.

"Albert," I say as our son Benjamin sits down on the piano bench beside me still holding my hand, "do you remember the night she died? Do you remember how she reached into her night table drawer, took out these pearls, handed them to me and said, 'You, Marty, are the saddest one of all my children and that's because,' she said, 'you're the purest, and the purest is always the saddest, so a word of advice,' she said as she put these pearls in my hand"—I'm remembering as my hand reaches up automatically to touch them—"'Don't let things get you down,' she said, 'let things make you TOUGH like me.' Then she said, 'Marty, wouldn't you rather have had Nancy for those five sweet years than to have never had her or the pain?" Then she closed her eyes, glowing in some kind of incandescent peace, released, finally free, her soul flying around the room big and beautiful—I'll never forget that night—it was like something seemed to leap out of her and soar, maybe to little Oscar Hornstien, who was waiting in the door jamb, grinning, with their precious son, who knows? I'm thinking as Benjamin moves closer to me on the piano bench in order to make room for the little dark-haired girl who came in with him.

When Nancy died Mrs. Hornstien never shed a

tear. For Albert and for me she became pure raw courage. As we fumbled, she grew only stronger, clearer, unleashing finally the full power of all her enormous strength. As Albert and I struggled to find a glimmer of light in this worst nightmare that again visited the Hornstien family, Mrs. Hornstien's tearless way of crying stopped absolutely, a final gift to us of the immensity of her love, only I was too young to know or to appreciate or to ever say thank you. "Marty," she would often say at the end, "don't you know by now THAT I KNOW EVERYTHING?" which I used to think was a ridiculous remark to which there was no answer, but she did know everything—absolutely everything—and the fact that I never said yes leaves me saddened, deeply saddened, I'm thinking as I wipe my eyes and nose on the back of my hand. "Ben," I say as I look at my son, who's still holding my hand, "do you remember," I ask him, "how your grandmother used to let you ride your new three-wheeler all around this whole enormous place? It used to worry me with all her art and all her priceless furniture and the grandfather clock at the end of the hall and all that heavy iron sculpture, but she'd bark whenever I'd say a word. 'SO WHAT,' she'd snap, 'what's a nick or scratch? It will only make everything more precious when all the children are grown.'"

"Mother," Benjamin interrupts as he lets go of my hand and gets up from the piano bench. "We have to run," he says, "but I wanted to bring Mary here before we couldn't get back in because I wanted her to see this place, this 'palace' like you used to call it," he smiles as he's prodding forward a little swarthy dark-haired girl, and as he's prodding her forward I notice he's holding her hand.

"Too bad," Ben says as he's pulling her in close to him, "it would have really been great to have gotten married here. We'll have missed it by only a couple of months."

"Married here?" I say. "Missed it by only a couple of months?"

"Yes," Benjamin says, smiling broadly. "Mother," he says, "this is Mary Fenkel. Mary," he says, "this is my mother."

"How do you do," I say as I stand up to get a better, closer, harder look at this skinny little girl with a lot of dark curly hair who's looking back at me, her big eyes stretched and staring.

"How do you do, Mrs. Hornstien," she says as she puts out her hand.

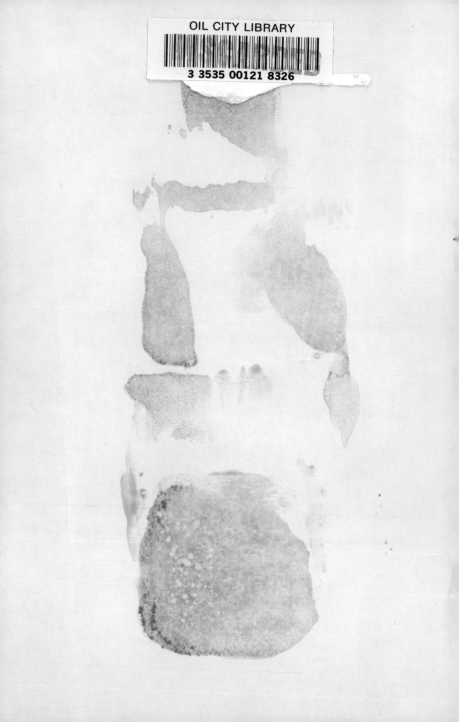